BRAINTREE
To renew
loan tel:
326057

28/11

2 4 NOV 2009

- 2 DEC 2011

CL11 TF(H)

PSL 1827H-12/94

Essex County Council
Libraries 3/03

GW00374350

30130 123765017

BY THE SAME AUTHOR
ALL PUBLISHED BY HOUSE OF STRATUS

ASK FOR RONALD STANDISH
THE BLACK GANG
BULLDOG DRUMMOND
BULLDOG DRUMMOND AT BAY
CHALLENGE
THE DINNER CLUB
THE FEMALE OF THE SPECIES
THE FINAL COUNT
FINGER OF FATE
THE ISLAND OF TERROR
JIM BRENT
JIM MAITLAND
KNOCK-OUT
MUFTI
THE RETURN OF BULLDOG DRUMMOND
SERGEANT MICHAEL CASSIDY R E
TEMPLE TOWER
THE THIRD ROUND

Use the Internet for FREE at all Essex Libraries

Essex County Council
Libraries

SAPPER

Bulldog Drummond

JOHN WALTERS

HOUSE OF
STRATUS

ESSEX COUNTY COUNCIL
LIBRARIES

Copyright by H C McNeile

All rights reserved. No part of this publication may be reproduced, stored in a retrieval system, or transmitted, in any form, or by any means (electronic, mechanical, photocopying, recording, or otherwise), without the prior permission of the publisher. Any person who does any unauthorised act in relation to this publication may be liable to criminal prosecution and civil claims for damages.

The right of H C McNeile to be identified as the author of this work has been asserted in accordance with sections 77 and 78 of the
Copyright, Designs and Patents Act 1988.

This edition published in 2001 by House of Stratus, an imprint of Stratus Holdings plc, 24c Old Burlington Street, London, W1X 1RL, UK.

www.houseofstratus.com

Typeset, printed and bound by House of Stratus.

A catalogue record for this book is available from the British Library.

ISBN 1-84232-553-1

This book is sold subject to the condition that it shall not be lent, resold, hired out, or otherwise circulated without the publisher's express prior consent in any form of binding, or cover, other than the original as herein published and without a similar condition being imposed on any subsequent purchaser, or bona fide possessor.

This is a fictional work and all characters are drawn from the author's imagination. Any resemblance or similarities to persons either living or dead are entirely coincidental.

CONTENTS

1	*The awakening of John Walters*	1
2	*A point of detail*	17
3	*My Lady of the Jasmine*	36
4	*The man-trap*	53
5	*Ebeneezer the goat*	72
6	*The pepnotised milk*	79
7	*Driver Robert Brown*	87
8	*The end of "Wipers"*	96
9	*The black sheep*	100
10	*The sixth drunk*	104
11	*The coward*	109
12	*"Will you take over his horse, sir?"*	118
13	*Morphia*	122
14	*The booby-trap*	137
15	*The passing of the seasick cow*	156

CHAPTER 1

The awakening of John Walters

Should you ever wander round the ranks of the North Sussex and inspect the faces of the men in that celebrated battalion, you will find that the majority are of the type bovine. They are a magnificent, if a stolid crowd, and their fighting record is second to none; but as might be expected in a regiment recruited largely from those who have been born and bred on the land, the prevalent expression of countenance is wooden. And in the rear rank of Number Three Platoon – at least that is where he used to exist beautifully – you will find the winner of the competition.

John Walters – the individual to whom I refer – was a great specimen of a man as far as his physical development was concerned; with regard to his brain the less said the better. Moreover, he looked it. He viewed life philosophically, if he viewed it at all; and the only thing which had ever been known to stir him into the slightest semblance of excitement was the unexpected addition of three more to his already numerous family circle. But the strain of endeavouring to work out the increase in separation allowance that this would give to the painstaking Mrs John proved too much for him, and with only the briefest of struggles, he relapsed once again into his normal torpor.

My story is of the awakening which came to our friend on a certain hot day in May. It was not permanent – he is now as comatose as ever – but while it lasted I am given to understand it

1

was quite a useful performance. And this was the way of it, on that morning in early summer.

For our scenery we must go to the front-line trenches in a certain district where mine craters grew and multiplied, and saps crept out, turning and twisting between the thrown-up mounds of earth on each side of them. In some places they were only ten yards apart – the English and the German sapheads – in others they were a hundred. But over the whole area there brooded that delightful sense of doubt and uncertainty which goes so far in cheering up its happy occupants. Complete ignorance as to where the next mine is going off, coupled with absolute certainty that it will go up somewhere, and that as far as you can see it's about your turn for attention, is a state of affairs at which only the most blue-faced pessimist could cavil.

And quite in agreement with that opinion was our friend John Walters on the morning of the day in question. At least it appeared so. To the casual observer the worthy John was quite content with his position; and if the thought ever crossed his mind that mines frequently went up in unexpected places, or that the saphead he was adorning was only fifteen yards away from the nearest Hun, it certainly was not reflected on his face.

Far from it. At the rise of the curtain he was lying sprawled on his back, and staring stolidly upwards.

He had been similarly occupied for the last hour, apathetically watching the stars pale gradually away, and the faint glow of dawn come stealing over the sky. Had he chosen to raise himself a little and look towards the east he could have seen the sun glistening like a gigantic orange ball, glinting through the thick white ground mist that covered everything; a sun that as yet had no heat in it. But John Walters did not choose to; he was quite comfortable, even if a little cold; and his mind was blank of any desire to be so energetic. Had anyone told him that this was the dawn of the most eventful day of his life, he would have contemplated the speaker without interest, spat with violence, and remarked in the fullness of time, " 'Oo be you a-gettin' at?"

After a while he shifted his position and ceased to gaze at the deepening blue above his head. He felt in each pocket in turn until he found an unpleasant-looking clay pipe whose bowl he carefully inspected. Apparently satisfied with what he saw he produced from another pocket a piece of plug tobacco; and having performed the mystic rite with due care and solemnity and the aid of a blunt knife, he thoughtfully rubbed the tobacco between his hands and stuffed his pipe with a square and dirty forefinger. Shortly after, the blue spirals of smoke ascending in the still summer air proclaimed that John was having his matutinal pipe.

Occasionally, when he thought about it, his eyes rested on a little piece of looking-glass on a stick set into a sand-bag in front of him – a glass tilted at an angle of forty-five degrees, which reflected the ground behind his back. It was the periscope at the end of the sap, and John was the sentry whose duty it was to look through it. The sap facing him ran back to the English front line. He could see the men asleep where it joined the trench twenty yards away – the others of the sap party; and every now and then he could see men going backwards and forwards in the fire trench. He settled himself more comfortably, and again the smoke curled upwards in the motionless air, while John ruminated on life.

Far be it from me to blame our friend for thus indulging in a little quiet introspection, aided and soothed by My Lady Nicotine. The occupation has much to commend it at suitable times and in suitable places. Unfortunately, the head of a sap on the flank of a continuous line of craters at five o'clock on a misty morning fulfils neither of these conditions. Further, there seems to be but little doubt that the review of his life was of such surprising dullness that the worthy John's head fell forward three or four times with the peculiar movement seen so often amongst those who are known as earnest church-goers. It occurs at intervals throughout the sermon, to be followed instantly by a self-conscious glance round to see if anyone noticed. Only there was no one at the moment to watch John, when his head first dropped slowly forward and his pipe fell unheeded to the ground – no one, that is, of whom our friend had any cognizance. But had his eyes been riveted on the periscope he would have seen a thing which would have galvanized even him into some semblance of activity.

Slowly, stealthily, a head was raised from behind a great hummock of chalky earth, a head surmounted by the round cloth cap of the German. Motionless the man stared fixedly at the little periscope – John's little periscope – then as if worked by a string the head disappeared; and when our hero, waking with a start, looked at the periscope himself with the guilty feeling that he had actually dozed on his post, once again it merely reflected the desolate, torn-up ground. But the German had seen John – and John had not seen the German, which is a dangerous state of affairs for solitary people in No Man's Land, when the range is about five yards.

It was just as our friend grunted and leaned forward to retrieve his pipe that it happened. Suddenly the saphead seemed to swarm with men who leaped into it out of the silent mists; a bullet-headed man seized John by the collar and yanked him out; the rest of the party seized the Mills bombs lying at the saphead, threw them at the sleeping piquet near the fire trench, and followed John's captor. In four seconds it was all over; the bombs burst in quick succession right amongst the piquet, and when an infuriated and excited officer came rushing up to find out what the devil was the matter, the only traces that remained were two dead men, a lance-corporal with a large hole in his leg, and – John Walter's unpleasant-looking clay pipe.

The next few minutes in our friend's life were crowded. Stumbling, half running, and ever conscious of a large and ugly revolver pointed at his stomach, he was driven over the uneven ground for twenty yards or so, and then without warning he tripped up and fell in a trench which he found in front of him, followed almost immediately by four panting Huns, who mopped their brows and grunted in a strange tongue. John was still completely bemused – the whole thing had been so sudden – and he sat for a while staring at the Germans.

"Gaw lumme!" he remarked at last, scratching his head in perplexity, "if you ain't the ruddy 'Uns. This 'ere's a fair box-up – that's wot it is."

Almost mechanically his right hand wandered to his jacket pocket in search of his pipe, only to receive a crashing blow on the elbow from a revolver butt.

" 'Ere – wot are you a-playing at?" His tone was aggrieved. "Danged if I ain't left my pipe in that there sap."

"English swine." One of the Germans spoke slowly, choosing his words with care. "You will later killed be."

"Go hon." John regarded him unmoved – he was still thinking about his pipe. "And look 'ere, guv'nor, I ain't 'ad no breakfast."

The German shook his head – our friend's accent was beyond him. Then seeming to realise that he was failing to hate sufficiently, he brought the butt of his rifle down with great force on John's foot, and drove him along the sap with the point of his bayonet. The procession turned along the fire trench – once again John tripped up; something hit him on the head, he felt himself falling down a timbered shaft, and then – no more.

Now, generally, when a man is taken prisoner he is removed with all possible speed to the rear, where he can be examined at leisure by men who know his language. At least, it is so in the case of German prisoners, and it is to be assumed it is so in the case of ours. Therefore our friend can deem himself lucky – though he certainly did not think so at the time – that the usual procedure was not followed in his case. Had it been, this more or less veracious narrative would never have been written; and our worthy John would even now be languishing in Ruhleben or some equally choice health resort.

He was roused from a sort of semi-stupor by a heavy kick in the ribs; and for a moment his mind was a blank – more even than usual. He was painfully aware that his head was very sore, and his stomach was very empty; and after he had completely grasped those two unpleasant facts he became further and even more painfully aware that a stoutly-booted German was on the point of kicking him again. He scrambled groaning to his feet; memories of the saphead had returned. The German pointed to the dug-out shaft; and when John again began remarking on the little matter of breakfast the stoutly-booted foot struck another portion of his anatomy even more heavily. Our hero, perceiving that the subject was unpopular, and encountering for the first time in his life the doctrine of *force majeure*, reluctantly began to climb the shaft. A bayonet prodded into the region of the last kick, and having let forth a howl, he climbed less reluctantly.

When he at last emerged blinking into the daylight of the trench, he looked, as is the way with those who are of the earth earthy, at the sun; and found to his surprise that it was late in the afternoon.

"Lumme, guv'nor!" he turned to the man behind him – "I ain't 'ad nothin' to eat all day. Not since last night, I ain't, an' then a perisher dropped me bread in the trench and trod on it."

His guard gazed at him impassively for a moment, and then kicked him again – in the stomach this time – while two men sitting on the fire-step laughed gutturally.

"English swine!" One of them mockingly held out a piece of bread, and then snatched it away again, as John was about to take it.

"Swine, yer ruddy self," he snarled, his slow bucolic temper beginning to get frayed.

But a rifle-butt in the ribs and a bayonet half an inch in his back showed him the unwisdom of such a proceeding; and he stumbled sullenly along the trench. It was lightly held, but everyone whom he did see seemed to take a delight in finding some hitherto unbruised part of his body to hit. At last, half sobbing with exhaustion and pain, he was propelled forcibly into another dug-out, where behind a table lit by candles there sat a man studying a map. He felt a hand like a leg of mutton seize him by the collar, force him upright, and then hold him motionless. After a few moments the man by the table looked up.

"What is the number of the battalion you belong to?" He spoke in perfect English.

"The Sixth." John's spirits rose at hearing his own language. "An', look 'ere, guv'nor, I ain't 'ad no – "

"Silence, you dog." The officer cried out something in German, and again the rifle-butt jolted into his ribs with such force that he groaned. "What division do you belong to?"

" 'Undred and fortieth." Our friend's tone was surly.

"Say 'sir,' when you speak to me. How long have you been in this part of the line?"

"I've been 'ere a month guv'nor – I mean, sir."

"Not you, dolt." The officer stormed at him. "Your division, I mean."

"Strike me pink, guv'nor, I dunno – I dunno, reely."

The wretched John's small amount of brain was rapidly going. Again the officer said something in German, and again an agonising jab took him in the ribs. It was a mistake, that last jab, if only the officer had known it. Given food and comparative kindness, John, out of pure ignorance of the harm he would be doing, might have racked his brains and said a lot. But that last unnecessary blow made him sullen – and when a man of that type gets sullen the Sphinx is talkative in comparison. For half an hour the cross-examination continued; were the men's spirits good, did they think they were winning, what was the food like?

And, ultimately, the officer told him in a furious voice that even for an Englishman he'd never met such a mutton-headed fool. With a last parting kick he was hurled into a corner and told to lie there.

Bruised in every limb, he crouched dazedly where he fell; with the whole of the slow, fierce anger of the countryman raging in his heart against the officer who still sat at the table. Occasionally men came in and saluted, but no word was spoken; and after a while John noticed that he seemed to be writing occasional sentences on pieces of paper. Sometimes an orderly came in and took one away; more often he crumpled them up and threw them on the floor. And then he suddenly noticed that the officer had a peculiar thing fitted round his head, with two discs that came over his ears.

"Come here." The terse command roused John from his semi-dazed stupor; he realised that the officer was speaking to him. "Put these over your ears, and tell me if you recognise who is speaking."

He handed a similar pair of discs over the table, which the Englishman clumsily put on his head. At first he could hear nothing distinctly but only a confused medley of chirrups and squeaks. Then suddenly quite distinctly there came a clear, metallic voice: "Halloa! is that the Exchange? Give me Don Beer."

"Gawd!" said John, in amazement. "Oo the 'ell is it?"

"That's what I want to find out," snapped the German. "Do you know the voice?"

"But it's in English." Our friend still gaped foolishly at this strange phenomenon.

"Do you know who it is, you dunderheaded idiot?" howled the officer, in a fury.

"Lumme; I dunno who it is. 'Ow should I?" John was aggrieved – righteously aggrieved. "Look out; the perisher's talking again."

"Is that you, Don Beer?" The thin voice, came once again clearly to John. "Oh! Is that you, Sally? Heard anything more about that man of yours they got this morning?" John noticed the officer was writing.

"Not a word, old dear. He was the world's most monumental idiot, so I wish 'em joy of him." Then once again the squeak chorus drowned everything else.

But John had heard enough. Regardless of the somewhat unflattering description of himself, unmindful of the officer's short laugh, he stared with amazement at the wall of the dug-out. For he had recognised that last voice.

"Who was that? D'you know?" The officer looked at John sharply.

"Well, I'm danged!" he muttered. "That last were old Sally – the old man."

"What old man, you fool?"

"Why, our colonel, guv'nor. There ain't more'n one old man."

"Oh!" The officer made a note. "So that was the colonel of your battalion, was it?"

"It wor, guv'nor – sir. An' if I might make so bold, sir, seeing as 'ow I 'aven't 'ad any food like since last night – "

"Silence, you worm." The officer got up, and struck him in the mouth. "We don't give food to Englishmen. Go back to your kennel. I may want you again."

He pointed to the corner, and resumed his seat, with the receivers of the listening apparatus over his ears once more. But John Walters was not interested – the entire performance left him cold. He wanted food, he wanted drink, and what German prisoners he'd seen had not wanted in vain. With a fierce smouldering rage in his heart, he lay hunched up, and his eyes never left the man at the table.

A far quicker-witted specimen than our friend might well have been excused for feeling a little dazed by the position in which he found himself. To be suddenly torn from the peaceful

9

monotony of ordinary trench life; to be removed forcibly from his friends, deprived of his breakfast and of his pipe; to be stunned by a blow on the head and on recovering consciousness to have the pleasure of hearing his colonel describe him as a most monumental idiot does not happen to everyone.

To the unfortunate John, still partially dazed and therefore slower on the uptake than ever, the situation was beyond solution. The only dominant thoughts which filled his mind were that he was hungry, and that he hated the man at the table. Every now and then he fell into a kind of stupor; only to come to again with a start, and see the same officer, with the same arrangement over his head, writing – writing. He was always writing, it seemed to John, and the constant stream of orderlies annoyed him.

God! how he hated that man. Lying in the corner, he watched him vindictively with his fists clenched and the veins standing out on his neck; then everything would go blurred again – his head would fall forward, and he would lie inert, like a log, practically unconscious. Men were moving; the officer was writing; he could still realise his surroundings dimly, but only with the realisation of light-headedness. At one time the dug-out seemed to be the tap-room of the "One Ton" – a hostelry largely patronised by our friend in the days of peace; while the officer who wrote took unto himself the guise of the proud owner. At another he thought he was in the battalion orderly-room and that the man behind the table was his CO. He tried to remember what his offence was, and why he was lying down, and why the escort was moving about instead of standing beside him. Then his brain cleared again and he remembered.

The exact act which cleared his senses was yet a further application of the boot by one of the dimly-moving figures. With a grunt John sat up and found beside him a hunk of unappetising-looking brown bread and a mug of water.

"Eat that up." The officer was speaking. "Then I shall want you again – so be quick."

John needed no second order. The fact that the bread was mouldy troubled him not at all; a hungry man looks not a gift loaf in the interstices. With a rapidity which would hardly be commended in a brochure on etiquette, he fell upon that hunk of bread, and having demolished it he felt better. It was just as he was washing down the last crumb with the last drop of water that he saw the officer at the table spring to his feet, while the two orderlies beside him also straightened up and stood to attention. He looked round to find the reason of the commotion, and found another officer standing near him regarding him malevolently. Somewhat refreshed by his meal, the worthy John came to the conclusion that he disliked the new arrival's face almost as much as his original enemy's, and returned the look with all the interest he was capable of displaying. It was not a judicious thing to do, but our friend was not a past-master in the higher forms of tact. Once again the dug-out became animated. Hitherto untouched areas of his anatomy received attention from two scandalised orderlies, and the ruffled dignity of the newcomer – a bull-necked man of unprepossessing aspect – was soothed. It was only John Walters' fury that increased until it almost choked him; but then to the other occupants of the dug-out John Walters' fury was a thing of no account. And but for the next little turn in the wheel of fate, their indifference was quite justifiable. He was unarmed: they were not. And no man, even though he possess the strength of ten is much use when an ounce of lead goes in at his chest and out at his back.

Completely disregarding the sullen prisoner, who stood breathing a little heavily just in front of an armed orderly, the two officers started an animated conversation. John, it is perhaps unnecessary to state, understood not one word; his school curriculum had not included German. Even had they spoken in English it is doubtful if their remarks would have conveyed much to him; though they furnished the reason of his temporary retention in his present abode.

"Any success?" The newcomer pointed to the receiver-discs lying on the table.

"Yes." The other officer held out one of the sets. "Try them on, and see what you think."

"Have you identified any of the speakers?"

The bull-necked man was adjusting his instrument.

"Only the colonel of the North Sussex for certain. That unmitigated fool" – he glared at John, who scowled sullenly back – "is too much of a fool to tell one anything. He is the thing we got this morning asleep in a sap."

The other nodded, listening intently, and for a while silence reigned in the dug-out.

To John the whole affair was inexplicable; but then a new and complicated listening apparatus might have been expected to be a bit above his form. He heard a salvo of shells come screeching past the entrance shaft, and realised with a momentary interest that they sounded much the same when they were English shells as they did when they were German. Then something hit the ground just outside with a thud, a something which he diagnosed correctly as a trench mortar bomb, and a second afterwards it exploded with a roar which deafened him, while a mass of dirt and lumps of chalk rained down the shaft.

The occupants of the dug-out betrayed no excitement; only John longed, with an incoherent longing, that another sixty-pounder would roll down the shaft next time before it exploded. He felt he would cheerfully die, if only those two accursed officers died at the same time.

Then came another salvo of shells and yet another; while in rapid succession the Stokes and Medium trench mortars came crumping down.

"A bit hactive tonight," thought John, listening with undisguised interest to the bursts outside. After all they were *his* bursts; he had every right to feel a fatherly pleasure in this strafing of the accursed Hun, even though his present position as one of them left much to be desired. A gentle smile of toleration spread over his face, the smile of the proud proprietor exhibiting his wares to an unworthy audience – and he glanced at the two officers. He noticed they were looking inquiringly at one another, as if debating in their minds whether it was an ordinary strafe or whether –

Suddenly the firing stopped, only to break out again as if by clockwork, a little farther away; and with that sudden change of target any doubts they had entertained as to the nature of the entertainment disappeared. They were being raided and they knew it; and any further doubts they may have still had on the matter were dispelled by a sudden shouting in the trench above them, coupled with the sharp cracks of bursting bombs.

To John the situation was still a little obscure. His brain creaked round sufficiently to enable him to realise that something had occurred to break up the happy meeting and cause feverish activity on the part of his captors. Various strange instruments were being hurriedly stowed away in a corner of the dug-out to the accompaniment of much guttural language; but his brain was still trying to grasp what had happened when he saw a thing which quickened his movements. Completely forgotten in the general rush he stood by the table, while the others darted backwards and forwards past him, carrying the instruments; and then suddenly the quickener arrived. Rolling down the steps there came a little black egg-shaped ball, which John recognised quicker than he had ever recognised anything before. It was a Mills bomb, and the pin was out. He was no bombing expert, but the habits of a Mills are known to most people who live with the breed. Four seconds – and then a most unpleasing explosion, especially when in a confined space like a dug-out.

So John acted. With a dispassionate grunt, he seized one of the orderlies who was brushing past him at the moment, all unmindful of the danger; and having picked him off the ground as if he were a baby he deposited him on the bomb, just in time. Barely had the dazed Hun alighted gently on the bomb when the bomb went off. So did the Hun, and the fun began. John's playful action had – amongst other good effects – prevented the lights from being blown out; and so at the trifling cost of one orderly he was in what is known as a strategically sound position. Moreover, he was in the most dreadful rage which had ever shaken his torpid disposition. Stunned by the sudden shock of the unexpected bomb and paralysed for the moment by the sight of the shattered man, the three Germans gazed foolishly at John Walters. And in that moment he went in at them. The second orderly fell like a stone with a blow on the point of the jaw which would have felled an ox; and only the two officers were left.

With a howl of rage the bull-necked officer rushed at him, and John grinned gently. He had no particular animosity against him: it was the other one he was after. So he hit him – once – and the bull-necked one slept, even like a little child.

Then for a moment or two John Walters stood still and contemplated the last occupant. Up above were his own pals, while down below his tormentor faced him alone. And they were on equal terms: they were both unarmed.

With a grunt of rage John caught him by the throat and shook him like a rat. All the fury pent up for so many hours came out as he bashed at his face with his fist. "No food, you dirty swine!" he muttered – bash, bash. "Kicked in me stummick, 'it in me mouth. I'll show yer – you perishin' 'Un! Come on upstairs and see the fun – come on, yer sausage-eating 'og!"

Bumping, heaving, pulling, he dragged the semi-conscious German up the shaft and with a mighty effort heaved him into the trench. There was no one in sight, though all around him bombs were going off – while away on each flank and behind the trench a ceaseless series of explosions merged into one continuous blast. John grunted again, and heaved the officer on to the parapet.

"Back 'ome with me this time, me beauty! Kicked in the stummick, no food since last night, and then a perisher trod on it. Gaw lumme, wot a life! Come on, yer swine!" and John got in the first real kick in the ribs with his boot. "Hup and hover. Gawd! – wot's that?"

Clear above the din there came from the British lines a discordant braying, which rose and fell like the wailing of a giant animal. It was the recall signal to the raiders.

" 'Op it, yer bla'guard, 'op it 'ard!" The bombing had died away, though the guns and mortars still roared. "In front of me, Mr 'Un – in front of me. Some of our boys be light on the trigger."

With the German firmly clasped to his chest the worthy John rushed him across No Man's Land. "It's Walters – John Walters," he bawled at the top of his voice – "and a 'Un." With a last final kick he sent him flying over the top of the parapet and fell in after him, breathing hard.

"What the devil?" An officer in the trench got up and gazed at the pair in amazement. "Who the hell are you?"

"John Walters, sir – and a 'Un." He scratched his head and mechanically kicked the recumbent German. "Get up, yer swine, and speak to the orficer!"

"Are you the fellow who was taken prisoner this morning?"

"Yes, sir, that's me." He gazed vindictively at his enemy. "An' not a bit of food since last night, and then some perisher trod on it. Gaw lumme, wot a life! Lucky as 'ow the boys come over, sir, or I wouldn't 'ave 'ad none at all – not with that there swine."

"Great Scott!" murmured the officer. This sudden appearance of the lost sheep temporarily unnerved him.

Not so John Walters. Having administered a final kick to the groaning Hun, he slouched moodily off into the night. His rage had abated – there only remained one thing to do before food. Absolutely unperturbed by various red and green lights which were now going up continuously from the German trenches as a signal for help, quite unmindful of the heavy shelling which had now started on our own trenches, our friend strode on to his appointed goal.

" 'Ave yer seen it lying about, mate?"

An astonished sentry peering into the darkness swung round sharply at the sudden voice behind him.

"Seen wot?" he demanded, crustily. "Wot are yer nosing abaht there for, and 'oo are yer, anyway?"

"John Walters, mate – John Walters, C Company."

"Lumme, but you was took prisoner this morning by the 'Uns!"

"I knows it – I knows all that. What I wants to know is – where's my ruddy pipe wot I dropped? Not a bit o' food since last night, and then some perisher trod on it. And now" – he was delving in the mud at the bottom of the sap – "danged if some other plurry perisher ain't been and gone and trod on this too!" By the light of a flare he ruefully examined two bits of a broken clay pipe. "Gaw lumme, wot a life!"

CHAPTER 2

A point of detail

"Hist!" The officer gripped the sergeant's arm just above the elbow, bringing his mouth close up to his ear. "Don't move." The words were hardly breathed, so low was the tense, sudden whisper, and the two men crouched motionless, peering into the darkness which enveloped them.

"Where, sir?" The sergeant slowly twisted his head till it was almost touching that of the man beside him; and he, too, whose normal voice resembled a human fog horn, scarcely did more than frame the words with his lips.

"Behind that mound of chalk. Several of them." The sergeant's eyes followed the line of the outstretched hand until they picked up the dark, menacing lump in the ground twenty feet away. Sombre, grim, apparently lifeless, outlined against the night sky – it appeared almost monstrous in size to the men who lay on the edge of a shell hole, with every nerve alert. A bullet spat over them viciously, but they did not alter their position – they knew they were not the target; and from their own lines came the sudden clang of a shovel. All around them the night was full of vague, indefinable noises; instinctively a man, brought suddenly into such a place and ignorant of his whereabouts, would have known that there were men all around him; men whom he could not see, men who flitted through the shadows bent on myster-ious tasks, men who moved silently, with eyes strained to pierce the darkness. Behind the German lines a trench tramway was in use; the metallic rumble of the trolleys on the iron rails came continuously from the distance. And suddenly from close at hand a man laughed…

"Do you see them?" Once again the officer was whispering, while he still grasped, almost unconsciously, the sergeant's arm. "There – there! Look!"

Two or three shadowy blobs seemed to move uncertainly above the edge of the chalk mound and then disappear again; and a moment afterwards, from almost on top of them, came a hoarse guttural whisper. The officer's grip tightened convulsively; the night of a sudden seemed alive with men close to them – pressing around them. Almost involuntarily he got up and moved back a few steps, still peering, straining to see in the inky blackness. Something loomed up and bumped into him, only to recoil with a muttered oath; and even as he realised it was a German he heard his sergeant's low voice from a few feet away. "Where are you, sir? Where are you?" The next moment he was back at his side.

"Get back your own way," he whispered; "we've bumped into a big patrol. Don't fire." And as he spoke, with a slight hiss a flare shot up into the night.

Now had it not been for that one untimely flare this story would never have been written. Indecent curiosity in other wanderers' doings in No Man's Land is an unprofitable amusement; while the sound of strafing, to say nothing of revolver shots, is calculated to produce a tornado of fire from all directions, administered impartially by friend and foe alike. Wherefore it is more than likely that but for the sudden ghostly light both the Englishmen would have got away. As it was, John Brinton, MC, Lieutenant in His Majesty's Regiment of the Royal Loamshires, found himself crouching in a slight dip in the ground and contemplating from a range of four feet no less than six Huns similarly engaged. There was the sharp crack of a revolver, a struggle, a muffled cry; then silence. Half a dozen more flares went up from each line; everywhere sentries peered earnestly towards the sound of the shot; a few desultory rifles cracked, and then the night resumed its whispering mystery. But at the bottom of the dip five Huns lay on the top of a stunned English officer; while the sixth lay still and twisted, with a revolver bullet in his brain.

Twenty minutes afterwards the sergeant, crawling warily on his belly, approached a saphead and after a brief word or two dropped in.

" 'Ave you seen Mr Brinton, sir?" he asked anxiously of an officer, whom he found in the sap, pessimistically smoking a cigarette – saps are pessimistic places.

"No." The officer looked up quickly. "He was out with you, wasn't he, Sergeant Dawson?"

"Yes, sir – on patrol. We'd just a-got to that there chalk 'ummock, when we ran into some of 'em. 'E said to me – 'Get back,' 'e said, 'your own way,' and then they put up a flare. I couldn't see 'im as I was lying doggo in a 'ole, but I 'eard a revolver shot about ten yards away. I looked round when the flare was out, but couldn't see him, nor 'ear him. So I thought 'e might 'ave got back."

"Pass the word along for Mr Brinton." The officer went out of the sap into the fire trench. "And get a move on with it." He stood for a few moments, looking thoughtful. "I hope," he muttered to himself, "I hope the old boy hasn't been scuppered."

But – the old boy *had* been scuppered. A runner failed to discover him in the trench; two strong patrols scoured the ground around the chalk 'ummock and drew blank. And so, in the fullness of time there appeared in the Roll of Honour the name of Lieut. John Brinton, of the Royal Loamshires, under the laconic heading of Missing, believed Prisoner of War, which is the prologue of this tale of the coalfields of France.

The part of the line in which the Royal Loamshires found themselves at the time of the unfortunate matter of John Brinton, MC, was somewhere south of La Bassée and somewhere north of Loos – closer identification is undesirable. It is not a pleasant part of the line, though there are many worse. The principal bugbears of one's existence are the tunnelling companies, who without cessation practise their nefarious trade, thereby causing alarm and despondency to all concerned. Doubtless they mean well, but their habit of exploding large quantities of ammonal at uncertain hours and places does not endear them to the frenzied onlookers, who spend the next hour plucking boulders from their eyes. In addition, there is the matter of sandbags. The proximity of a mine shaft is invariably indicated by a young mountain of these useful and hygienic articles, which tower and spread and expand in every direction where they are most inconvenient. I admit that, having placed half the interior of France in bags, the disposal of the same on arriving in the light of day presents difficulties. I admit that the fault lies entirely with the harassed and long-suffering gentleman who boasts the proud title of "spoils officer." I admit – But I grow warm, in addition to digressing unpardonably. The trouble is that I always do grow warm, and digress at the mention of sandbags.

In part of the Loamshires' front line, mining activity was great. A continuous group of craters stretched along No Man's Land, separating them from the wily Hun, for half the battalion front – a group which we will call Outpost. The name is wrong, but it will serve. To the near lips of each crater a sap ran out from the front line, so that merely the great yawning hole lay between the saphead and the corresponding abode of the Germans on the other lip. Each night these sapheads were held by a small group of men armed with Verey lights, bombs, bowie knives, and other impedimenta of destruction; while between the saps the trench was held but lightly – in some cases not at all. The idea of concentrating men in the front line has long been given up by both sides.

If, therefore, one strolls along the firing line – a tedious amusement at all times – it is more than likely that one will find long stretches completely deserted. The scene is desolate; the walk is strangely eerie. Walls of sandbags tower on each side, in some cases two or three feet above one's head; the clouds go scudding by, while the shadows of a traverse dance fantastically as a flare comes hissing down. The Hun is thirty yards away; the silence is absolute; the place is ghostly with the phantoms of forgotten men. And sometimes, as one walks, strange fancies creep into one's brain. Relics of childish fears, memories of the bogey man who waited round the end of the dark passage at home, come faintly from the past. And, foolish though it be, one wonders sometimes with a sharp, clutching pang of nervous fear – What is round the next corner?

Nothing – of course not. What should there be? The night is quiet; the trench is English. The next party is forty yards farther on; the voices of the last still come softly through the air. And yet – and yet – ! But I digress again.

Now not one of the least of all the crimes of those responsible for the disposal of the underworld of France, when it comes to the surface in sandbags, is the following. (Lest any one may think that I am writing a textbook, I would crave patience.) Be it known, then, that to keep out a bullet some four feet of earth are necessary. Less than that and the bullet will come through and impinge with great violence on the warrior behind. This fact is well known to all whose path in life leads them to the trenches; but for all that Tommy is a feckless lad. In some ways he bears a marked resemblance to that sagacious bird, the ostrich; and because of that resemblance, I have remarked on this question of disposing sandbags in terms of grief and pain. The easiest thing to do with a sandbag in a trench, if you don't want it, is to chuck it out. Human nature being what it is, the distance chucked is reduced to a minimum – in other words, it is placed on the edge of the parapet. More follow – and they are placed beside it on the edge of the parapet; which causes the inside of the parapet to increase in height, but *not* in thickness. In other words, after a while the top two or three layers of bags, though looking perfectly safe from the inside, are not bullet proof. Which Tommy knows – but…well, I have mentioned the ostrich.

Now this state of affairs existed in one or two places behind Outpost craters. There were spots where the top of the parapet was not of sufficient thickness to keep out a rifle bullet. And it was just by one of these spots that the Company Commander, going round one night, suddenly stumbled on something that lay sprawling at the bottom of the trench – an unmistakable something. It lay half on the fire step and half off, midway between two saps, and the head sagged back helplessly. He switched on his torch, and having looked at the huddled form, cursed softly under his breath. For it was his senior subaltern, and a bullet had entered his head from behind just above the neck. It had come out at his forehead, and we will not specify further.

"Stretcher bearers at once." He went back to the group he had just left. "Mr Dixon has been shot through the parapet, farther up."

"Killed, sir?" The NCO in charge was in Dixon's platoon.

"Yes." The Company Officer was laconic. "Brains blown out. It's that damned parapet – one sandbag thick. What the hell's the use of my speaking?"

He had had a trying day, and his tone may be excused. "You sit here and you do nothing. The whole company are a set of cursed lazy loafers."

Seeing that the men were getting an average of six hours' sleep the remark was hardly fair, but, as I said, the day had been a trying one and this had been the last straw. He strode back again to the dead subaltern, muttering angrily.

"Poor old man," he whispered gently, lifting the legs on to the fire step and bending over the still form. "Poor old man; you've solved the Big Mystery by now, anyway." The light of his torch fell on the dead man's face, and he shuddered slightly: a bullet can do a lot of damage. Then he climbed on the fire step and looked over the parapet. It was a place where the spoils party had been particularly busy; and though the Company Officer was full six foot, he could only just see over the top; as a fire step it was useless to anyone but a giant from a freak show.

"Hallo! what's happened?" A voice behind him made him turn round.

"That you, Dick? Poor little Jerry Dixon been shot through the parapet – that's what's happened." He got down and stood at the bottom of the trench beside the second-in-command. "The three top layers there are only one bag thick." Once again his language became heated.

"Steady, old man," Dick Staunton puffed steadily at his pipe, and looked at the body lying beside them. "Were you with him when he was hit?"

"No. Came round visiting the sentries and found him lying there dead."

"Oh!" He switched on his torch and continued smoking in silence. Suddenly he bent forward and peered closely at the shattered head. "Give me a hand for a minute. I want to turn the boy over."

Faintly surprised, he did as he was bid.

In silence they turned the body over, and again there was silence while Staunton carefully examined the spot where the bullet had entered.

"Strange," he muttered to himself after a few moments, "very strange. Tell me, Joe" – his voice was normal again – "exactly how did you find him? What position was he in?"

"He was half sitting on the fire step, with his head in the corner and his legs sprawling in the bottom of the trench."

"Sitting? Then his face was towards you."

"Why, yes. Is there anything peculiar in the fact? He'd probably just been having a look over the top, and as he turned away to get down he was hit through the sandbags in the back of the neck. His head was a bit forward as he was getting down, so the bullet passed through his head and out of his forehead."

In silence they turned the boy over again and covered his face with a pocket-handkerchief.

"You're too much of a blooming detective, you know, old man. Much police work has made thee mad," laughed the Company Commander. "What else can have happened?"

"I'm no detective, Joe." The other man smiled slightly. "But there are one or two small points of detail which strike me, though I can make nothing out of them, I admit. First – his height. He's six inches shorter than you, and yet you could barely see over the top. Therefore, what was he doing trying to look over the parapet here of all places? Secondly, the way he fell. A man killed instantaneously, and shot through the back of his head, would in all probability pitch forward on his face. You say his face was towards you, and that he was sitting in the corner of the traverse." He paused to fill his pipe.

"Go on," said the Company Commander curiously. "You interest me."

"The third point is one on which I admit that I am doubtful. The bullet wound is clean. Now I am inclined to think – though I don't know – that a bullet passing through a chalk bag would become jagged, and would not be travelling straight when it continued its flight. However, I don't attach much importance to that. And the fourth and last point is almost too trifling to mention. Do you notice anything peculiar about his uniform?"

The listener flashed his torch over the dead officer. "No," he said at length. "I can't say that I do. Except that one of his regimental badges is missing. I suppose you don't mean that, do you?" The Company Officer laughed irritably.

"I do," returned the other quietly. "It's a point of detail, even if a little one." He looked thoughtfully at the man in front of him. "Do I strike you as a callous sort of devil, old man?"

"You seem to be treating the boy rather on the line of a specimen for improving your deductive powers."

"Perhaps you're right." Staunton turned away. "But I didn't mean it that way – quite. Sorry, Joe; the boy was a pal of yours?"

"He was."

"God rest his soul!" The second-in-command spoke low. Then, with a final salute to the youngster whose soul had gone to the haven of fighting men, he turned away and vanished into the night.

The next day the Company Commander came round to Battalion Headquarters.

"My two best subalterns," grunted the Colonel in disgust, "within two days. Very annoying. Good boys – toppers both of them. You'd go quite a way, Dick, before you bettered Brinton and Dixon."

"You would," affirmed the second-in-command. "Quite a way."

"And with all your theorising last night, old man," remarked the Captain slyly, "we both forgot the obvious solution. He got on the fire step, found he couldn't see over – so he clambered up on top. Then, when he was getting down, he was hit, and slithered into the position I found him in."

Staunton regarded the speaker through a haze of tobacco smoke. "I wonder," he murmured at length. "I wonder."

He did not state that during the morning he had made a point of interrogating Jerry Dixon's servant. And that worthy – an old and trusted soldier – had very positively denied that either of the Pelicans Rampant, which formed the regimental badge, had been missing from his master's coat the previous evening.

"Now Mr Brinton's coat, sir," he remarked thoughtfully, "that did 'ave a badge off, that did. But 'is servant!" He snorted, and dismissed the subject scornfully.

As I say, the Major did not mention this fact. After all, it was such a very small point of detail.

To the frivolous-minded, Dick Staunton was at times the cause of a certain amount of amusement. Originally in the Army, he had left it when a junior captain, and had settled down to the normal life of a country gentleman. By nature of a silent disposition, he abominated social functions of all sorts. He hunted, he fished, and he shot, and spent the rest of his time studying the habits of the wild. And as always happens to a man who lives much with nature, his mind gradually got skilled in the noticing of little things. Small signs, invisible to the casual observer, he noticed automatically; and without being in any sense a Sherlock Holmes, he had acquired the habit of putting two and two together in a manner that was, at times, disconcertingly correct.

"Points of detail," he remarked one evening in the dug-out after dinner, "are very easy to see if you have eyes to see them with. One is nothing; two are a coincidence; three are a moral certainty. A really trained man can see a molehill; I can see a mountain; most of you fellows couldn't see the Himalayas." With which sage remark he thoughtfully lit his pipe and relapsed into silence. And silence being his usual characteristic he came into the Battalion Headquarters dug-out one evening and dropped quietly into a seat, almost unnoticed by the somewhat noisy group around the table.

"Afternoon, Dickie." The Sapper officer looked up and saw him. "D'you hear we're pinching your last recruit? Jesson – this is Major Staunton." He turned to a second lieutenant in the Royal Loamshires beside him as he made the introduction.

"How d'you do, sir." Jesson got up and saluted. "I've only just got over from England; and now apparently they're attaching me to the RE, as I'm a miner."

He sat down again, and once more turned his attention to that excellent French illustrated weekly without which no officers' mess in France is complete. Lest I be run in for libel, I will refrain from further information as to its title and general effect on officers concerned.

For a few moments Staunton sat watching the group and listening with some amusement to the criticisms on those lovely members of the fair sex so ably portrayed in its pages, and then his attention centred on the revolver he was cleaning. Jesson, a good-looking, clean-cut man of about twenty-nine or thirty, was holding forth on an experience he had had in Alaska, which concerned a woman, a team of dogs, and a gentleman known as One-eyed Pete, and as he spoke Staunton watched him idly. It struck him that he seemed a promising type, and that it was a pity the Tunnellers were getting him.

"Haven't you got enough disturbers of the peace already," he remarked to the Tunnelling officer, "without snatching our ewe lamb?"

"We are at full strength as a matter of fact, Major," answered an officer covered with chalk; "but they do some funny things in the palaces of the great. We often get odd birds blowing in. I've been initiating him all this morning into the joys of Outpost."

"And how is jolly old Blighty?" remarked the Adjutant. "Thank Heaven! leave approaches."

"About the same." Jesson helped himself to a whisky-and-soda. "Darker than ever, and taxis an impossibility. Still I dare say I shall be glad enough to go back when my first leave comes due," he added with a laugh.

"Is this your first time out?" asked Staunton.

"Yes." Jesson unbuttoned his burberry and took out a cigarette case. Outside the dusk was falling, and he bent forward to get a light from the candle flickering on the table in front of him. "The very first time. I've been on Government work up to now."

It was at that moment that a very close observer might have noticed that Dick Staunton's pipe ceased to draw with monotonous regularity: he might even have heard a quick intake of breath. But he would have had to be a very close one – very close indeed; for the next instant he was again speaking and his voice was normal.

"I suppose you've been at the depot," he hazarded. "Who are there now?"

"Oh, the usual old crowd," answered Jesson. "I don't expect you know many of them though, do you, Major? Ginger Stretton in the 14th Battalion – do you know him by any chance?"

"No, I don't think I do." His face was in the shadow, but had it been visible a slightly puzzled frown might have been seen on his forehead. "I suppose they still make all you fellows on joining go to the regimental tailor, don't they?"

Jesson looked a trifle surprised at the question. "I don't think they are as particular as they were," he returned after a moment. "Personally I went to Jones & Jones." He casually buttoned up his mackintosh and turned to the Tunneller. "If you're ready I think we might be going. I want to see about my kit." He got up as he spoke and turned towards the entrance, while at the same moment the Sapper rose too. "I'd like to drop in again, sir, sometimes, if I may." He spoke to the shadow where Staunton had been sitting.

"Do." Jesson gave a violent start, for the voice came from just behind his shoulder. Like the hunter he was, Dick Staunton had moved without a sound, and now stood directly between Jesson and the door. "But don't go yet. I want to tell you a story that may amuse you. Have some tea."

"Er – won't it keep till some other time, Major? I'm rather anxious to see about my kit."

"Let the kit keep. Sit down and have some tea."

"What the devil has come over you, Dickie?" The Adjutant was looking frankly amazed. "You aren't generally so loquacious."

"That's why tonight my little whim must be honoured," answered Staunton with a slight smile. "Sit down, please, Jesson. It's quite an amusing little yarn, and I would like your opinion on it."

"No hope for you, old boy. Dickie has turned into a social success." The Adjutant laughed and lit a cigarette, and once again became immersed in his paper.

To the casual observer the scene was a very normal one. Four men in a dug-out, yarning and reading; while outside the occasional whine of a shell, the dirty deeds of a Stokes gun, the noises of the trenches filled the air. Nothing unusual, nothing out of the way except – something, an indefinable something. As the Sapper said afterwards there must have been something tangible in the atmosphere – else why did his pulses quicken. He glanced at the Adjutant sitting opposite him engrossed in his book; he looked at Staunton across the table – Staunton, with a slight smile on his lips – and his eyes fixed on Jesson. He looked at Jesson beside him – Jesson, whom he had met that morning for the first time. And all he noticed about Jesson was that his left knee twitched ceaselessly…

He ran over in his mind the day's work. He had met him at about eleven that morning, wandering along the line support with an officer in the Loamshires whom he knew well, who had hailed him and introduced Jesson.

"A recruit – a new recruit," he had said, "for your atrocious trade. He's just left old pimple-faced Charlie, who was writing returns in triplicate as usual."

Now pimple-faced Charlie was his own Major, who habitually did write returns in triplicate; wherefore, after a few remarks of a casual nature in which he elicited the fact that Jesson was a mining engineer and had suddenly been ordered while waiting at the base to join the 940th Tunnelling Company, he took him in tow and showed him round the mine galleries.

Mining work was very active in the sector. Four or five small mines and one big one were going up in the near future, so the tour of inspection had been a long one. That his companion was not new to the game was obvious from the outset; and his pertinent inquiries anent cross-cuts, listening galleries, and the whole of the work in hand had shown that he was keen as well. Altogether a promising recruit, he had mused: quite a find – keen and able, two qualities which unfortunately do not go hand in hand quite as often as one would like. And now Staunton and this find of his were facing one another in silence across the plank table of the dug-out; Jesson, with an expression of polite indifference as befitted a subaltern compelled to listen to a senior officer's story which he didn't want to hear; Staunton, with an enigmatic smile. Then of a sudden Staunton spoke.

"Have you ever studied the question of the importance of matters of detail, Jesson?" he remarked quietly to the impassive figure facing him across the table.

"I can't say that I have, sir," answered the other, politely stifling a yawn.

"You should. A most interesting study. My story concerns points of detail. The imperative thing is to be able to sort out the vital points from all the others; then piece them together, and arrive at the right answer."

"It must be very easy to be led astray, I should imagine; and arrive at the – er – wrong one." Jesson concealed a smile, and waited for the Major to continue.

"Yes and no. It's all a matter of practice." Staunton's imperturbable voice was as quiet as ever. "And anyway, it's only in peace time that it matters very much whether one is right or wrong. Nowadays! Well – *à la guerre comme à la guerre*." He smiled gently. "But my story. I want you, as an impartial observer, just arrived, with an unbiased mind, to tell me if you think my joining up of two or three points of detail is a sound one. Both these officers know the points of detail, so your opinion will be more valuable than theirs.

"A few nights ago our battalion had one of those unfortunate little contretemps that so often happen in war. A subaltern of ours, John Brinton by name, went out on patrol, and never returned. An exhaustive search in No Man's Land failed to discover his body; so we were reluctantly compelled to conclude that he was in German hands; whether alive or dead we don't know. There we have the first fact in my case. Now for the second.

"Two nights after that another of our subalterns was killed in a way which struck me as peculiar. I will not weary you with all the various little points that led me to believe that the bullet which killed him did not come from the trenches opposite; I will merely say that his position, his height, and the depth of the trench were the most obvious. And granted that my conclusions were correct, strange as it might appear at first sight, his death must have been caused at close quarters, possibly in the trench itself."

"Good Lord!" muttered the Adjutant, who was now listening with interest. "What do you mean?"

"Two facts, you see," went on Staunton quietly. "And they would have remained unconnected in my mind – Brinton's capture and Dixon's death – but for a small point of detail. Dixon's jacket was without the left regimental badge when his body was found. His servant knows he had them both earlier in the day. On the contrary, Brinton had lost his left regimental badge for some time. Am I interesting you?"

"Profoundly, thank you, sir." The man opposite smiled amiably.

"I'm glad of that; it's an interesting problem. You see the significance of that small point about the badge, the way in which it connects very intimately Brinton's capture and Dixon's death. So intimately, in fact, does it connect them, that one is almost tempted to assume that the man who killed Dixon was the man in possession of Brinton's uniform. Are you with me so far?"

"The evidence seems a trifle slight," remarked Jesson.

"Quite true; the evidence is very slight. But then, it often is. Everything up to date turns on the question of the badge. Let me reconstruct a possible – only possible, mark you – story, based on the supposition that my badge theory is correct. A German who speaks English perfectly is given a nice warm uniform taken from a captured British officer. Then he is told to go over to the British lines and see what he can find out. He comes one night; perfectly easy; no trouble; until walking along the front line he meets another officer – alone: an officer of the same regiment as that whose uniform he is wearing. Unavoidable; in fact, less likely, to raise suspicion with the frequent changes that occur if he goes to the same regiment than if he went to another. But something happens; either the other officer's suspicions are aroused, or the German does not wish to be recognised again by him. The trench is quiet; an occasional rifle is going off, so he does the bold thing. He shoots him from point-blank range – probably with a Colt. As he stands there with the dead officer in front of him, waiting, listening hard, wondering if he has been heard, he sees the two badges on the officer's coat. So, being a cool hand, he takes off the left one, puts it on his own coat, and disappears for a time. Quite easy; especially when the trenches are old German ones."

"Really, Major, you seem to have made a speciality of detective fiction. As you said, I suppose your theory is possible."

Jesson spoke casually, but his eyes for the first time left the face of the man opposite him and roved towards the door. For the first time a sudden ghastly suspicion of the truth entered the Sapper's brain; and even as it did so he noticed that Staunton's revolver – the cleansing finished – pointed steadily at Jesson's chest.

"I am glad you think it possible. To render it probable we must go a bit farther. The essence of all detective stories is the final clue that catches the criminal, isn't it?" The revolver moved an inch or two into prominence.

"Good Lord, Dickie! Is that gun of yours loaded?" cried the Adjutant in alarm. For the first time he also seemed to become aware that something unusual was happening, and he suddenly stood up. "What the devil is it, Major? What have you got that gun on him for?"

"For fun, dear boy, for fun. It's part of the atmosphere. We've got to the point, haven't we, where – in my story, of course – the German dressed in Brinton's uniform comes into the English lines. Now what sort of a man would they send in this part of the line, where mining activity is great? I continue the theory, you see; that's all."

He looked at Jesson, who made no reply; though without cessation he moistened his lips with his tongue.

"A miner." The Adjutant's voice cut in. "Go on, for God's sake."

"Precisely – a miner. The second point of detail; and two points of detail are a strange coincidence – nothing more. Only – there is a third."

"And three are a moral certainty, as you've often said." The Adjutant once again bent across the table and spoke softly. "Are you fooling, Dickie – are you fooling? If so, the joke has gone far enough."

But the Sapper's eyes were fixed on a leg that twitched, and they wandered now and then to a neck where – even in the dim light of a candle – he could see a pulse throbbing – throbbing.

"It's not a joke," he said, and his mouth was dry. "What is the third point of detail, Dickie?"

"Yes, what is the third point of detail, sir?" Jesson's voice was steady as a rock. "I am very interested in your problem." He raised his hands from the table and stretched them in front of him. Not a finger quivered, and with a sublime insolence he examined his nails.

To the Sapper there occurred suddenly those lines of Kipling,

> "For there is neither East nor West, border nor
>   breed nor birth,
> When two strong men come face to face though
>   they come from the ends of the earth."

He *knew* now; he realised the man beside him was a German; he knew that the sentence of death was very near. What the clue was that had given the man away he hardly thought about – in fact, he hardly cared. All he knew was that death was waiting for the man beside him, and that his hands were steady as a rock.

Quietly Staunton leant forward and undid Jesson's mackintosh. Then he sat back and with his finger he pointed at a spot above his left breast-pocket. "You have never been out to the front, you say; your coat is a new one by Jones & Jones; and yet – until recently – you have been wearing the ribbon of a medal. What medal, Jesson, what medal? It shows up, that clean patch in the light. John Brinton went to Jones & Jones; and John Brinton had a Military Cross."

For a full minute the two men looked into one another's eyes – deep down, and read the things that are written underneath, be a man English or German. Then suddenly Jesson smiled slightly and spoke.

"You are a clever man, Major Staunton. When will the rifle practice take place?

Thus it ended, the play of which John Brinton's disappearance formed the prologue. But before the curtain rang down on the epilogue the German told them one or two little things: that John Brinton was alive and well; that the existence of Ginger Stretton, to whom he had alluded so glibly, had only become known to him from a letter in Brinton's coat; that the peculiarities of pimple-faced Charlie had been forced on him by his guide before they met the Sapper.

"In fact," as the Adjutant remarked, "the fellow was almost too good a sportsman to – " But that's the epilogue.

A file of men; a watery sun just starting its day's work; a raw, chilly morning. In front – a man: a man with a white disc of paper pinned over the heart.

A word of command; a pushing forward of safety catches; a volley; a finish.

CHAPTER 3

My Lady of the Jasmine

The Kid staggered wearily along the road through the blinding rain. Dodging between the endless stream of traffic, which moved slowly in both directions, now stopping for ten minutes, now jolting forward again for a couple of hundred yards, he walked on towards where he thought his battalion was. The last Staff officer he had seen had told him that, as far as he knew, they had pulled out to rest in some dug-outs about four miles farther on – dug-outs which had only recently been taken from the Germans. To start with he had got on to a lorry, but when darkness fell, and the total progression had been one mile, he decided to walk and save time. Occasionally the lights of a car shone in his face, as its infuriated occupant broke every rule of the Somme roads by double banking; that is, trying to pass the vehicles in front. But at last the traffic wore thinner as the road approached the front line, and an hour and a half after he had left the lorry, it stopped altogether, save for pack-mules and squelching men. The rain still sogged down, and – ye gods! the Kid was tired. Away into the night there stretched a path of slippery duckboards, threading its way between shell holes half filled with water. Men loomed up out of the darkness and went past him, slipping and sliding, cursing below their breath. A shower of sparks shot up into the air from a dug-out on his right, and a great lobbing flare away in the distance lit up the scene for a second or two with a ghostly radiance. It showed the Kid the only other near occupant of the reclaimed territory at the moment: a mule, whose four hoofs stuck stiffly out of a shell hole – pointing at him, motionless. With a shudder he moved on along the duck-walk. After all he was but a kid, and he was almighty tired.

For three days he seemed to have been on the run without closing his eyes. First the battalion had gone over the top; then they had worked like slaves consolidating what they'd won; afterwards he had been sent for because of his knowledge of French and German to go back to Divisional Headquarters; and then he had come back to find the battalion had moved. And any who may have tried walking five or six miles by night in heavy rain to an unknown destination along some of the roads east of Albert, will bear out that it is a wearisome performance. When to these facts is added the further information that the age of the boy was only eighteen, it will be conceded that the breaking-point was not far off.

Now I have emphasised the physical condition of the Kid, as he was known to all and sundry, because I think it may have a bearing on the story I am going to relate. I am no expert in "ologies" and other things dealing with so-called spiritualistic revelations. I might even say, in fact, that I am profoundly sceptical of them all, though to say so may reveal my abysmal ignorance. So be it; my thumbs are crossed. This is not a controversial treatise on spiritualism, and all that appertains thereto. One thing, however, I will say – in my ignorance, of course. Until some of the great thinkers of the world have beaten down the jungle of facts beyond our ken, and made a track – be it never so narrow – free from knaves and charlatans, it is ill advised for Mrs Smith or Lady de Smythe to believe that Signor Macaroni – *neé* Jones – will reveal to them the secrets of the infinite for two pounds. He may; on the other hand, he may not. That the secrets are there, who but a fool can doubt; it is only

Signor Macaroni's power of disinterested revelation that causes my unworthy scepticism.

And so let us come back to the Kid, and the strange thing that happened in a recently captured German dug-out on the night of which I have been writing. It was just as he had decided – rain or no rain – to lie down and sleep in the mud and filth – anywhere, anything, so long as he could sleep – that suddenly out of the darkness ahead he heard the Adjutant's voice, and knew that he had found the battalion. With almost a sob of thankfulness at the unexpected finish of his worries, he hailed him.

"Hallo! is that you, Kid?" The Adjutant loomed out of the darkness. "We thought you were lost for good. Are you cooked?"

"I'm just about done in," answered the boy. "Where is B Company?"

"I'll show you. It's the hell of a place to find even by day; but you've got 'some' dug-out. Beer, and tables, and beds; in fact, it's the first dug-out I've seen that in any way resembles the descriptions one reads in the papers."

"Well, as long as I can get to sleep, old man, I don't care a damn if it's the Ritz or a pigsty." The Kid plucked his foot from a mud-hole, and squelched on behind the Adjutant.

Now much has been written about German dug-outs – their size, their comfort, the revolving bookcases, the four-poster beds. Special mention has frequently been made of cellars full of rare old vintages, and of concreted buttery hatches; of lifts to take stout officers to the ground, and of portable derricks to sling even stouter ones into their scented valises. In fact, such stress has been laid upon these things by people of great knowledge, that I understand an opinion is prevalent amongst some earnest thinkers at home that when a high German officer wishes to surrender he first sends up two dozen of light beer on the lift to placate his capturers, rapidly following himself with a corkscrew. This may or may not be so; personally, I have had no such gratifying experience. But then, personally, I have generally been hard put to it to recognise the dug-outs of reality from the dug-outs of the daily papers. Most of them are much the same as any ordinary, vulgar English dug-out; many are worse; but one or two undoubtedly are very good. In places where the nature of the ground has lent itself to deep work, and the lines have been stagnant for many moons, the Huns have carried out excellent work for the suitable housing of their officers. And it was down the entrance of one of these few and far between abodes that the Kid ultimately staggered, with the blessed feeling in his mind of rest at last. Round a table in the centre sat the other officers of B Company, discussing the remains of an excellent German repast. As he came in they all looked up.

"The lost sheep," sang out the Captain cheerfully. "Come on, my kidlet, draw up, and put your nose inside some beer."

"Not a bad place, is it?" chimed in the Doctor, puffing at a large and fat cigar of Hun extraction. "Excellent cellar of rare old ale, cigars of great potency – real genuine Flor de Boche – a picture gallery of – er – a pleasing description, and a bed. What more can man desire?"

"Private MacPherson does not approve, I fear me, of the pictures," chuckled the senior subaltern. "I heard him muttering dark things about 'painted Jezebels,' and 'yon scarlet women of Babylon.'"

"It must be very dreadful for all concerned to go through life with a mind like MacPherson's." The Doctor was examining his cigar doubtfully. "There is an obstruction in this. It's either going to explode with great force in a minute, or else I'm coming to the motto. Hi! you blighter – " he jumped up hurriedly to avoid the stream of beer that shot across the table from the Kid's overturned glass.

"Idiot child." The Company Commander roused himself from his gentle doze to contemplate the delinquent. Then he smiled. "Man, he's asleep; the boy's beat to a frazzle."

"Aye, you're right. Tim, come off that bed; the Kid is fair cooked. Wake up, infant." The Doctor shook him by the shoulder. "Wake up. Take off your boots, and then get down to it on the bed."

The Kid sat up blinking. "I'm very sorry," he said after a moment. "Did I upset the beer?"

"You did – all over me," laughed the Doctor. "Get your boots off and turn in."

"I'm so cursed sleepy." The Kid was removing his sodden puttees. "I've walked, and walked, and I'm just about –" He straightened himself in his chair, and as he did so the words died away on his lips. With a peculiar fixed look he stared past the Doctor into the corner of the dug-out. "My God!" he whispered at last, "what are you doing here?"

A sudden silence settled on the mess, and instinctively everybody, including the Doctor, glanced towards the corner. Then the Doctor turned once more to the boy, and his glance was the glance of his profession.

"What's the matter, Kid?" His tone was abrupt, even to curtness. "Did you think you saw something?"

"I thought – I thought –" The boy passed his hand over his forehead. "I'm sorry – I must have been dreaming. It's gone now. I suppose I'm tired." But his eyes still searched the dug-out fearfully.

"What did you think you saw?" asked the Doctor shortly.

"I thought I saw –" Once again he stopped; then he laughed a little shakily. "Oh! it doesn't matter what I thought I saw. Damn it! I'm tired; let me turn in."

The Doctor's eye met the Company Commander's over the table, and he shrugged his shoulders slightly. "Dead beat." His lips framed the words, and he returned to the contemplation of his cigar, which was not doing all that a well-trained cigar should.

The Kid stood up and glanced round the mess at his brother officers a little shamefacedly; only to find them engrossed – a trifle ostentatiously – in their own business. "I'm sorry, you fellows," he blurted out suddenly. "Forgive me for being such a fool; I suppose I'm a bit tired."

The Doctor took him firmly by the arm, and led him towards the bed. "Look here, old soul," he remarked, "if you wish to avoid the wrath of my displeasure, you will cease talking and go to bed. Everyone knows what it is to be weary; and there's only one cure – sleep."

The Kid laughed and threw himself on the bed. "Jove!" he muttered sleepily; "then it's a pleasant medicine, Doctor dear." He pulled a blanket over his shoulders; his head touched the pillow; his eyes closed; and before the Doctor had resumed his seat the Kid was asleep.

It seemed only a minute afterwards that he was awake again, staring into the dim-lit dug-out with every sense alert. He was conscious first of a faint elusive scent – a scent which was new to him. His mind wandered to the scents he knew – Chaminade, Mystérieuse, Trèfle Incarnat – but this was different. Delicate, sensuous, with the slightest suggestion of jasmine about it, it seemed to permeate every part of him. Vaguely expectant, he waited for something that he knew must happen. What it would be, he had no idea; he felt like a man waiting for the curtain to rise on a first night, when the music of the overture is dying away to a finish. He experienced no fear: merely an overwhelming curiosity to witness the drama, and to confirm his certainty about the owner of the scent. In his mind there was no doubt as to who she was. It was the girl he had seen in the corner as he was taking off his puttees: the girl who had looked at him with eyes that held the sadness of the world and its despair in them; the girl who had vanished so quickly. Her disappearance did not strike him as peculiar; she would explain when she came. And so the Kid waited for the drop-scene to lift.

It struck him as he glanced round the dug-out that the furniture had been moved. The table seemed nearer the wall; the chairs were differently arranged. Instead of the remnants of a finished meal, papers arranged in neat piles met his eye. The place looked more like an office than a mess. Suddenly he stiffened into attention; steps were coming down the entrance to the dug-out. A man came in, and with a gasp the Kid recognised a German soldier. He strove to shout – to warn his brother officers who he knew were peacefully sleeping in valises on the floor; but no sound came. His tongue stuck to the roof of his mouth; he could only watch, rigid and motionless.

The German moved to the hanging lamp, and turned it up till a bright light flooded the dug-out.

"Now," the Kid's brain was racing, "he must see them. My God! they must have got back during the night."

But no. The German servant moved towards the cupboard which contained the food, brushing so close to the bed that the Kid could have touched him with ease as he passed. Very cautiously he raised his head as he saw the man, his back turned, fumbling on the shelves, and looked round the room. Then with the icy hand of terror clutching at his heart he lay back again. The room was empty; his brother officers had gone – murdered probably – and with him it could only be a question of moments before he too was discovered.

For an instant he had a wild idea of hurling himself upon the German: of taking him unawares – of trying to escape. Then the soldier turned: the opportunity had passed, and once again the silent spectator on the bed lay rigid. The servant, stolid and unemotional, moved heavily about the dug-out, laying the table for a meal. Once it seemed to the Kid that he looked straight at him; he could have sworn that he must have been seen; and yet – apparently not. The man gave no sign, and it occurred to the Kid that perhaps he was lying in the shadow. Stealthily he wormed himself even nearer to the wall: impelled by the instinct of self-preservation that he would put off to the last possible moment the inevitable discovery. And hardly had he edged himself in against the wall, when with a sinking heart he heard voices outside; voices which spoke in German. With only the servant to tackle, somehow he had not felt so hopeless; now he knew the end had come.

Two officers entered, wiping the perspiration from their foreheads. One from his badges of rank he recognised as a Colonel – the other was a Lieutenant; and the discussion was – as far as their difference of rank allowed – obviously of an acrimonious nature. The Kid listened intently; thanking Heaven, not for the first time in his life, that someone with a grain of common sense had had him taught French and German by a method other than the Public School one. The predilection of his aunt's gardener for pens, ink, and paper would not have helped him much in that conversation.

"Beer, you fool," grunted the Colonel to the stolid servant. "Then, go."

Impatiently he waited till the orderly's footsteps died away, and then he turned savagely on the other officer.

"I tell you, Lieutenant Rutter, we *must* know," he snarled. "A girl – what is a girl, when big issues are at stake? There are many more girls, Lieutenant Rutter; many more girls. Be very careful lest not only does this one die, but you also meet with an accident. Dead men cannot make love to those other girls." He banged his fist on the table and glared at the Lieutenant, who was staring moodily in front of him.

"I know that, Excellency," he returned after a moment. "But there is a proverb about bringing a horse to the water and not being able to make him drink."

"Bah! There are methods, my friend, of drowning the brute with water, if it won't drink willingly. And those methods will have to be adopted in this case."

"They are doubtless effective in killing the horse; but they will not lead us very much farther in our inquiries."

"Which is the reason why I have allowed you so much rope. I know as well as you do that willing information is worth ten times as much as when it is forced. You have made love to the girl, you have been playing the fool for six weeks with her, and we are no nearer than when we started." He sneered openly. "Since when have we become so dilatory, my friend? You seem to have lost your form with the fair sex."

The Lieutenant flushed, and his fist clenched. "Don't mention those others. I love this girl."

"No doubt thinking of marriage?" The sneer was even more in evidence.

"Yes, Excellency, I am thinking of marriage." His voice was ominously quiet.

"I am afraid, Lieutenant Rutter, it will remain in the beautiful and nebulous realms of thought, unless –" He paused and drained his beer ostentatiously, though all the while his eyes never left his companion's face.

"Unless," repeated the Lieutenant drearily, "she agrees to do some charming and honourable spying work for us on the other side of the lines."

"You speak very strangely, Lieutenant Rutter." The little pig eyes of the senior officer glinted menacingly. "Have a care."

"Pardon, Excellency. For the moment I forgot." With a weary gesture he got up. "I will ask her this morning." He looked at his watch. "She should be here very soon."

"Then I will await the result of your interview through here." The Colonel moved to a door half concealed by a curtain. "You shall have your turtle dove, Rutter, in peace and quiet." He chuckled harshly. "You know what we want?"

"By heart, Excellency."

"And you remember that her brother the Comte is not really dead. For our purposes he is a prisoner."

"I am not likely to forget; but I warn you, Excellency, I have but little hope of succeeding."

The Colonel's jaw shut like a vice. "Then God help you both, my friend; God help you both." His voice was soft, but horribly menacing; and as the curtain dropped behind him, the Kid, who had been listening spellbound, understood for the first time the type of man who represented Prussian militarism.

Instinctively his heart warmed towards the Lieutenant, who with a weary gesture of despair was resting his head on his arms. He was young, clean cut, almost an Englishman to look at, save for his close-cropped bristling hair; and, moreover, he was up against it. All the Kid's sporting instincts rose within him. Boche or no Boche this was not the type of swine who launched gas and liquid fire on a horror-struck world. Forgetful of everything he was on the point of going over to him and telling him to stick it out, when his eyes rested on the entrance. And there was the girl: the girl he had seen in the corner, the girl of the jasmine scent. For a while she stood watching the bowed figure at the table, and then she tip-toed across to him and laid her hand on his head.

With a quick start he looked up, and into his face there came the light of all the ages, the light of the man for the woman he loves.

"Marie," he whispered hoarsely. "Marie – *que je t'adore*." He caught her to him and kissed her on the lips. Then, with a bitter groan, he pushed her away and sat down again.

"Fritz, what is it?" she cried in wondering tones. "You sent for me, my dear. Why? I came; but it is not right for me to come to you here – in your dug-out."

"I was ordered to send for you, my Marie." His French was pure if guttural.

"Ordered!" An adorable look of amazement came on her face. "And you liked not this order, my Fritz. But why? It is not right for me to be here, I know; but now that I have come, it is very nice, *mon ami*. Why do you look so glum?"

For a while he did not reply, but paced the dug-out with long, uneven steps. And the Kid, watching his lady of the jasmine, saw her bite her lips, as a look of puzzled fear came into her great round eyes. At last the man paused in front of her and took her roughly by the arms, so that she cried out.

"You love me, Marie?" he demanded hoarsely. "You love me enough to marry me when this accursed war is over?" His voice sank over the last few words, and he glanced, half fearfully, at the curtained door.

"But of course, my Fritz," she answered softly. "You have been good to me, and you are different to these others. Mon Dieu! they frighten me – those harsh, brutal men; but they have been good to me and the little mother for your sake. It is terrible, I suppose – a French girl and a German officer; but the little god Love, *mon ami*, he laughs at the great god Mars – sometimes. Poor little me – I cannot help myself." She laughed adorably, and the Kid laughed with her. She seemed to him like the spirit of the Spring, when the bluebells are flowering and the world is young. But on the German's face there was no answering smile. It was set and stern, and imprinted with a look of such utter hopelessness that the Kid, who saw it over the girl's shoulder, almost cried out with the pain of it.

"Do you love me enough, Marie," he went on at length, "to do a big thing for me – a very big thing?"

"That depends on what it is." She spoke gaily, but the Kid could see her body stiffen slightly. "I'm no good at big things."

"Will you go to Paris for me?" His voice was dull and jerky.

"Paris!" She gazed at him in amazement. "But how, and why?"

"It will be easy to get you there." He seized on the part of her question which postponed for a few seconds the hideous thing he was to ask her. "We can arrange all that quite easily. You see – " He rambled on with the method of making plans for the journey, until he caught her eyes, and the look in them made his faltering words die away to a dreadful silence.

"And why do you want me to go to Paris, Fritz?" Her voice was hardly above a whisper.

Twice he essayed to speak; twice he failed to do more than falter her name. Then with a gasping cry he took her in his arms and kissed her passionately. "They shan't," he muttered; "by God! they shan't." And it was as the Kid watched the scene, with parted lips and quickened breath, that the curtain moved aside, and he saw the Colonel, like an evil spirit, regarding the pair with cold malevolence.

"Delightful!" he remarked after a few moments of cynical observation; "delightful! Lieutenant Rutter, you are to be congratulated. Mademoiselle – you are charming; all that my young friend has said, and more."

He moved forward and stood by the table, while Marie – her face as white as death – clung to her lover. "Who is he, Fritz, this ugly old man?" she whispered, terrified.

"Permit me to introduce to you..." Fritz forced the words from his dry lips, only to stop at the upraised hand of the other.

"My name, dear young lady, is immaterial," he remarked genially. "Just an ugly old man, who has had no time to bask in the sunshine of the smiles of your charming sex." He sat down and lit a cigar. "So you are going to become a German's wife! Ah! Fritz, my boy, you're a lucky dog! You'll have to guard your Marie carefully from the rest of the garrison, when we have finally won and the war is over." He gave a grating laugh, and blew out a cloud of smoke.

"What do you want of me?" asked Marie, in a terrified whisper, looking at him like a bird at a snake.

"A little service, my dear young Fräulein to be – a little service to the Fatherland. You must not forget that Germany is now your country in spirit, if not in actual truth. You are pledged to her just as you are pledged to your Fritz – in fact, he being an officer, the two are one and the same thing." He smiled again, and waved his cigar gently in the air. "And not only will your service benefit the country that you have chosen as your own, but it will benefit you, because it will bring the end of the war, and with it your marriage, closer."

He paused to let the words sink in, but she still watched him fascinated.

"One thing more." His eyes gleamed dully through the haze of smoke as he fixed them on her. "Unless this little service is fulfilled, though it won't make any difference to the ultimate result as far as Germany is concerned, it will make a very considerable difference as far as you and – er – Fritz are concerned."

"What do you mean?" The girl hardly breathed the words.

"I mean there will be no marriage. Painful – but true."

The Kid watched the young officer's arm tighten convulsively round her waist – and began to see red. Then the harsh guttural voice continued. "Well, now, without wasting any more time, let us come to the point. I had proposed to let Lieutenant Rutter explain things to you; but – er – from one or two things I overheard, it struck me he might not make them clear." The beady eyes came slowly round to the Lieutenant. "That is why I interrupted." Once again he stared at the trembling girl. "To be brief, Mademoiselle Marie, we anticipate an attack – a big attack – by the English. We have good information that it is coming in this neighbourhood."

The Kid pricked up his ears; what the devil was the man talking about? "We have every reason to hope that Ovillers, Fricourt, Thiepval are impregnable; at the same time – in war – one never leaves things to chance." The Kid's astonishment turned to stupefaction; he himself had been in the storming of Ovillers. "And the chance," continued the imperturbable voice, "in this matter is the probable action of the French – your charming compatriots – er – compatriots that *were*, Fräulein. We anticipate this offensive in about a month or six weeks; and the matter on which we require all the confirmation we can is whether the French, after their hideous losses at Verdun, can play any important part in this operation of the enemy. That is where you can help us."

For a moment there was dead silence, and then the girl turned her stricken face to the man beside her. "Dear God!" she muttered, "is this why you made love to me? To make me a spy?"

"Marie – no, on my honour; I swear it!" Forgetful of the man sitting at the table Fritz stretched out his hand in an agony of supplication.

"Lieutenant Rutter." With a snarl the Colonel stood up. "You forget yourself. I am speaking. A truce to this fooling. Mademoiselle" – he turned again on the girl – "we have other things to do beside babble of love. Call it spying if you will, but we want information, and you can help us to get it – *must* help us to get it."

"And what if I refuse?" Superbly she confronted him; her voice had come back; her head was thrown up.

"In the first place you will not marry Lieutenant Rutter; and in the second place – have you heard that the Comte de St Jean was taken prisoner at Verdun?"

"Philippe. Oh, monsieur, where is he?" The girl threw herself on her knees before him. "I implore you – he is my only brother."

"Indeed. Well, if you desire to see him again you will carry out my suggestion. Otherwise – " he paused significantly.

"Oh, you could not! You could not be so cruel, so vile as to harm him if he is a prisoner. It would break my mother's heart."

"Mademoiselle, there is nothing which I would scruple to do – nothing – if by so doing I advanced the glorious cause of our Fatherland." The man's small eyes gleamed with the fire of a fanatic; revolting though he was, yet there was an element of grandeur about him. Even the Kid, watching silently from the bed, felt conscious of the power which seemed to spring from him as he stood there, squat and repulsive, with the lovely French girl kneeling at his feet. He saw her throw her arms around his knees, and turn up her face to his in an agony of pleading; and then of a sudden came the tragedy.

Discipline or no discipline, a man is a man, and Fritz Rutter had reached the breaking-point. Perhaps it was the sight of the woman he loved kneeling at the feet of one of the grossest sensualists in Europe, perhaps – But who knows?

"Marie," he cried hoarsely, "it's not true. Philippe is dead; they cannot hurt him now. Get up, my dear, get up." With folded arms he faced the other man as the girl staggered to her feet. Heedless of the blazing passion on the Colonel's face, she crept to Fritz and hid her face against his chest. And as she stood there she heard the voice of her tormentor, thick and twisted with hate.

"For that, Lieutenant Rutter, I will have you disgraced. And then I will look after your Marie. Orderly!" His voice rose to a shout as he strode to the door.

"Goodbye, my love." Fritz strained her to him, and the Kid saw her kiss him once on the lips. Then she disengaged herself from his arms, and walked steadily to where the Colonel still shouted up the entrance. Outside there was the sound of many footsteps, and the girl paused just behind the cursing maniac in the door.

"So you will look after me, will you, monsieur?" Her voice rose clear above the noise, and the man turned round, his malignant face quivering. The Kid watched it fascinated, and suddenly he saw it change. "I think not," went on the same clear voice; and the guttural cry of fear rang out simultaneously with the sharp crack of a revolver.

"My God!" Rutter stood watching the crumpling figure as it slipped to the ground in front of the girl; and then with a great cry he sprang forward. And with that cry, which seemed to ring through his brain, there came the power of movement to the Kid.

He hurled himself off the bed towards the girl – his girl – his lady of the jasmine. But he was too late. The second shot was even truer than the first, and as her head hit the floor she was dead.

Regardless of Rutter the Kid knelt down beside her, and as he did so, he got it – in the face.

"What the blazes are you doing?" roared an infuriated voice. "Damn you! you young fool – you've nearly killed me."

Stupefied the boy looked around. The same dug-out; the same officers of B Company; the same beer bottles; but where was the lady of the jasmine? Where was the man who lay dead in the doorway? Where was Rutter?

He blinked foolishly, and looked round to find the lamp still burning and his brother officers roaring with laughter. All, that is, except the Doctor on whose stomach he had apparently landed.

But the Kid was not to be put off by laughter. "I tell you it happened in this very dug-out," he cried excitely. "She killed the swine in the doorway there, and then she killed herself. This is where she fell, Doc, just where you're lying, and her head hit the wall there. Look, there's a board there, nailed over the wall – where her head went. Don't laugh, you fool! don't laugh – it happened. I dreamed it. I know that now; but it happened for all that – before the big advance. I tell you she had light golden hair – ah! look." The Doctor had prised off the board, and there on the wall an ominous red stain showed dull in the candlelight. Slowly the Doctor bent down and picked up something with his fingers. Getting up he laid it on the table. And when the officers of B Company had looked at it, the laughter ceased. It was a little wisp of light golden hair – and the end was thick and clotted.

"Tomorrow, Kid, you can tell us the yarn," said the Doctor quietly. "Just now you're going to have a quarter-grain of sleep dope and go to bed again."

The following evening the officers of B Company, less the Kid, who was out, sat round the table and talked.

"What do you make of it, Doc?" asked the Company Commander. "Do you really think there is anything in the Kid's yarn? I mean, we know he dreamed it – but do you think it's true? I suppose that tired as he was he would be in a receptive mood for his imagination to run riot."

For a long while the Doctor puffed stolidly at his pipe without answering. Then he leaned forward and put his hand in his pocket.

"Imagination, you say. Do you call that imagination?" He produced the lock of hair from a matchbox. "Further, do you call that imagination? I found it under the pillow this morning." On the table beside the matchbox he placed a small pocket-handkerchief, and from it there came the faint, elusive scent of jasmine. "And last of all, do you call that imagination? I found it in one of the books yonder." He placed an old envelope in front of him, and the others crowded round. It was addressed to Ober-Lieutenant Fritz Rutter.

CHAPTER 4

The man-trap

Should you, in the course of your wanderings, ever run across Brigadier-General Herbert Firebrace, do not ask him if he knows Percy FitzPercy. The warning is probably quite unnecessary: not knowing FitzP yourself, the question is hardly likely to occur to you. But I mention it in case. One never knows, and Herbert will not be prejudiced in your favour if you do.

As far as I know, the story of their first – and last – meeting has never yet been told to the world at large. It is a harrowing tale, and it found no place in official *communiqués*. Just one of those regrettable incidents that fade into the limbo of forgotten things, it served as a topic of conversation to certain ribald subalterns, and then it gradually disappeared into obscurity along with Percy FitzPercy. Only it took several months for the topic to fade; Percy beat it in about ten seconds.

Before the war Percy had been, amongst other things, an actor of indifferent calibre; he had helped a barman in Canada, carried a chain for a railroad survey, done a bit of rubber-planting, and written poetry. He was, in fact, a man of many parts, and cultivated a frivolous demeanour and an eyeglass. Unkind acquaintances described him as the most monumental ass that has yet been produced by a painstaking world; personally, I think the picture a trifle harsh. Percy meant well; and it wasn't really his fault that the events I am about to chronicle ended so disastrously. Unfortunately, however, he was unable to get the General to see eye to eye with him in this trifling matter; and so, as I have already said, Percy beat it in about ten seconds.

The whole trouble started over the question of mantraps. "If," remarked a Sapper subaltern one night after the port had been round more than once – "If one could construct a large conical hole like an inverted funnel in the front-line trench, so that the small opening was in the trench itself, and the bottom of the funnel fifteen or twenty feet below in the ground, and if the Huns came over and raided us one night, one might catch one or two." He dreamily emptied and refilled his glass.

"By Jove, dear old boy" – Percy fixed his eyeglass and gazed admiringly at the speaker – "that's a splendid idea! Sort of glorified man-trap – what! – dear old thing."

"That's it, Percy, old lad. Why don't you make one next time you're in the trenches?" The speaker winked at the remainder of the party.

" 'Pon my soul, dear old man, I think I will." Percy was clearly struck with the idea. "Cover the hole, don't you know, with trench-boards by day, and have it open at night. Great idea, old sport, great idea!"

"You could go and fish for them in the morning with a sausage on the end of a string," murmured someone. "Get 'em to sing the 'Hymn of Hate' before they got any breakfast."

"Or even place large spikes at the bottom on which they would fall and become impaled." The first speaker was becoming bloodthirsty.

"Oh, no, dear old chap! I don't think an impaled Hun would look very nice. It would be quite horrible in the morning, when one started to count up the bag, to find them all impaled. Besides, there might be two on one stake." Exactly the objection to the last contingency was not clear; but after dinner attention to such trifles is of secondary importance.

"Percy inaugurates new form of frightfulness," laughed the Major. "May I be there when you catch your first!"

The conversation dropped; other and more intimate topics anent the fair ones at home took its place; but in the mind of Percy FitzPercy the germ of invention was sown. When he went back to his battalion that night, in their so-called rest-billets, he was thinking. Which was always a perilous proceeding for Percy.

Now it so happened that his part of the line at the moment had originally belonged to the Hun. It was a confused bit of trench, in which miners carried on extensively their reprehensible trade. And where there are miners there is also spoil. Spoil, for the benefit of the uninitiated, is the technical name given to the material they remove from the centre of the earth during the process of driving their galleries. It is brought up to the surface in sandbags, and is then carried away and dumped somewhere out of harm's way. In reality it is generally stacked carefully in the trenches themselves, thereby completely blocking all traffic; which is by the way.

But after mining has been in progress for some time, and various craters have been blown and sapped out to, and after trench mortars have "strafed" consistently for many months and torn the original surface of the ground to pieces, the actual position of the trenches themselves become haphazard. They cease in many cases to bear the slightest likeness to the ordinary trenches of commerce; they become deep gorges in mountains of sandbags. I have sometimes wished that those officers who apparently write home to devoted bands of female workers asking for more sandbags would get in touch with me instead. I shall be delighted to let them have anything up to five million, all filled, by return; which is again by the way.

To return to Percy. In his part of the front sandbags grew like pebbles on a shingly beach; and from time to time fresh cuts off the trenches were opened to allow for further expansion in the sandbag family. The existing front line in one place had started life as a cut off the old trench, and had gradually been taken into use as a permanency, and it was at this point that he stumbled on the great discovery which was destined to cause all the trouble. How he first stumbled is not recorded; but early one morning Percy FitzPercy could have been seen like a terrier with his nose down a rabbit-hole, lying flat at the bottom of the trench, peering into a noisome and foul-smelling cavity underneath him.

"My dear old boy," he remarked enthusiastically to a brother subaltern, who was watching the proceeding coldly, "it's an old German dug-out; I'm *certain* it's an old German dug-out."

"I don't care a damn if it is," answered the other, without enthusiasm. "It stinks like a polecat, and is undoubtedly full of all creeping things. For heaven's sake, let's go and get something to eat."

Slowly and reluctantly Percy allowed himself to be led away, thinking deeply. Only the week before had the Hun attempted a raid and actually entered the trench close to the spot in question, and here was apparently a ready-made man-trap should he do so again. After breakfast he would explore his find; after breakfast he would himself set to work and labour unceasingly. As I have said, Percy FitzPercy meant well.

It is possible that lesser men might have been deterred by the unpromising results of that exploration. Descending gingerly through the hole, which had been widened sufficiently to allow of the passage, Percy switched his torch around the cavity he found himself in. Above his head long rounded timbers, side by side and touching one another, formed the roof, which was in good condition, save in the centre, where the blue sky shone through the hole he had entered by. In one corner stood a bedstead covered by a moth-eaten blanket, while all over the floor crumbling sandbags and old clothes and equipment gave it the appearance of a rag-and-bone shop. In one place the wall had fallen in, a mound of chalk filled the corner, and from a score of vantage points elderly rodents watched with increasing disfavour this unexpected human invasion.

Up above in the trench the disfavour was repeated in that picturesque phraseology for which Thomas is famous.

"Wot are you a-doing 'ere?" An incensed sergeant rounded the corner, and gazed wrathfully at three privates, each armed with a spade and wearing gas helmets. "Wot 'ave you got them 'elmets on for?" He approached the fatal hole, and recoiled slightly. "Gaw-lumme! Wot's that smell?"

"Percy," answered a sepulchral voice. "Our little Perce."

"Wot yer mean – Percy? Wot's that 'ole?" A cloud of dust at that moment rose through it, and he recoiled still farther. "Oo's down there?"

"Percy," answered the same sepulchral voice. "Percy FitzP carrying hout a reconaysance in force. 'E's found a 'Un smell factory, and 'e's fair wallowing in it."

At that moment a voice came gently through the opening. "I say, you fellahs, just come down here a moment, and bring your shovels – what?"

A face, covered with a fine coating of blackish-grey dust, popped out of the bottom of the trench. "We're fairly going to catch the old Hun before we've finished."

With a choking gasp the sergeant lost all self-control and faded rapidly away, while the three privates slowly and reluctantly followed the face through the hole.

It was fortunate – or possibly, in view of future events, unfortunate – that during the next two hours no responsible individual came along that particular piece of front line. Incidentally there was nothing surprising in the fact. In most places, especially during the day, the front line is held but lightly by isolated posts, which are visited from time to time by the company or platoon commander, and more rarely by the Colonel. On this particular occasion the CO had already paid his visit to the scene of activity. The company commander was wrestling with returns, and Percy himself led the long-suffering platoon. And so without hindrance from any outsiders the fell business proceeded.

Volumes of evil-smelling dust poured out into the trench, punctuated from time to time with boots, a few rats who had met with an untimely end, some unrecognisable garments, and large numbers of empty bottles. An early investigation had shown the indomitable leader that the old shaft which had led down to the dug-out in the days when it was used was completely blocked up, and so the hole through the roof was the only means of entrance or exit. Moreover, the hole being in the centre of the roof, and the dug-out being a high one, there was no method of reaching it other than by standing on the bed or the decomposing chair. Once the bird was in there, granted the bed had been removed, there was therefore no way by which he could get out without being helped from above. And so with joy in his heart the indefatigable Percy laboured on, what time three sweating privates consigned him to the uttermost depths of the pit.

Now one may say at once that Percy had all the makings in him of the true artist. Having decided to stage his performance, he had no intention of letting it fail through lack of attention to detail. Life in the front trenches is not at any time an enlivening proceeding; the days drag wearily by, the nights are full of noises and Verey lights – and this particular part of the line was no exception to the general rule. So our hero was not distracted by mundane influences or stress of work from elaborating his scheme. In addition, once the miasma had subsided, and the idea had been explained to them, the three supers became quite keen themselves. It was one of them, in fact, who suggested the first detail.

" 'Ow are we to know, sir," he remarked, as they sat resting on an adjacent fire-step after three hours' strenuous exhuming, "that supposing two of the perishers fall through the 'ole they won't escape? Two men could get out of that there place without no bed to 'elp 'em."

"By Jove, yes!" Percy scratched his forehead and left furrows of white in the general darkness. "By Jove, yes; you're quite right – what? Break one's heart to lose the blighters, don't you know. You're a doocid clever fellow to think of that, Jenkins."

"Tomkins, sir," murmured the originator of the brainwave, slightly abashed by the unexpected praise.

"We might," remarked another of the world's workers, thoughtfully sucking his teeth – "we might 'ave a trapdoor, a 'eavy one, to let down over the 'ole once they was in."

"Yus – and 'ow are we to know when they is in?" The third member of the party proceeded to justify his existence. "They won't come over 'ere and fall into the 'ole and then shout to us to let down the trap." He thoughtfully lit a Woodbine. "The 'Un will be strafing if there's a raid on, and there'll be the 'ell of a beano going on, and no one won't never 'ear nothing."

With which sage aphorism he relapsed into silence, and a gloom settled on the meeting.

"By Jove, you fellows, we must think of something! We must pull up our socks and think – what? After we've spent all this time clearing the bally place out we must really think of something – by Jove!" Percy gazed hopefully at his three supers, but it seemed that their contributions to the conversation were at an end, and for a space silence reigned, broken only by the gentle lullaby of the tooth-sucker.

"We might," remarked Tomkins at length, after a period of profound thought, " 'ave a trip-wire, wot would ring a gong."

"That's it – that's it! 'Pon my word, you're a doocid clever fellow, Thomson, doocid clever fellow – what?" Percy became enthusiastic. "Ring the gong where the fellah is who lets down the door. He lets down the door, and we bag the Hun. Dam' good idea!"

"I don't believe in no gongs," remarked the musical one scornfully. "No – nor trip-wires either." He eyed his audience pugnaciously.

"But, my good fellah – er – what do you believe in?" Percy's spirits were sinking.

"Tins, china, cups and saucers, plates, old saucepans – anything and everything wot will make a noise when the 'Un falls on it. That's the ticket, sir," he continued, with gathering emphasis as he noted the impression he was causing. "Lumme – a trip-wire: it might break, or the gong mightn't ring, or the blighter mightn't 'ear it. Wiv china – every step he took 'e'd smash anuvver pot. Drahn a rum jar 'e would. But – a trip-wire!" He spat impartially and resumed his tune.

"By Jove, that's a splendid idea!" The mercurial Percy's face shone again. "Splendid idea! Fill it full of old tins and china – what? And when we hear the second fellah hit the floor and start breakin' up the home we can pull the string and let down the trapdoor. Splendid idea! Doocid clever of you, 'pon my soul it is!"

"And where do you think of getting the china from?" Tomkins, fearing that his mantle of doocid cleverness was descending upon the tooth-sucker, eyed him unconvinced. "I wasn't aware as 'ow there was a penny bazaar in the neighbour-hood, nor yet a William Whiteley's."

"Yes, by Jove," chirped Percy, "where do we get it all from? We shall want lots of it, too, don't you know – what?"

"Get it?" The suggester of the idea looked scornful and addressed himself to Tomkins. "There ain't no bully tins in the perishing trenches, are there? Ho no! An' there hain't no china an' bits of glass and old cups and things in that there village about 'alf a mile down the road? Ho no! I reckon there's enough to fill twenty 'oles like that there." Once again the oracle resumed his hobby.

"Splendid!" Percy jumped to his feet. "The very thing! We'll do it this next company relief, by Jove! Now, boys, two more hours. We just want to get the bedstead out and straighten things up, and we'll be all ready for the dinner-service – what?"

Now there was another thing in which Percy FitzPercy showed that he had the makings of a true artist. He fully appreciated the value of secrecy in presenting his performances to the public at large. True, all his platoon were bound to find out, and the remainder of the company had a shrewd idea that something was afoot. But one does not walk along trenches – especially in the front line – for pleasure; and beyond a casual inquiry as to what new form of insanity he was up to now, the company commander was not interested in Percy's doings. Now that the place had been cleared out, the opening was covered during the day by a trench-board carefully stolen from the nearest RE dump; while the members of the platoon assiduously collected old tin and china utensils, both great and small, which were thrown into the cavity and arranged tastefully by the stage-manager.

At night the trench-board was removed, and after careful weighting with two dud shells, a piece of rail, and the stalk of a sixty pound trench-mortar bomb, it was placed on edge beside the hole. It was so arranged that it leaned slightly inwards, and was only kept from falling by a cord which passed in front of it and which was attached to two screw pickets – one on each side. The hole itself was covered with a sack. So much for the scenery.

The stage directions were equally simple. The curtain rises on a German raid. Noises off, etc.; the flashes of guns, the bursting of rum jars, the dazzling brilliance of flares lighting up the lowering night. On the entrance of the Hun into the trench (if he did), a watch would be kept on the hole (if anyone was there to watch). On the sound of the first crash of breaking china, no action. On the sound of the second crash of breaking china, Percy himself (if alive) or a substitute (if not), would dash forward and cut the string. The trapdoor would fall; and then, having repelled the Hun, they could return and examine the bag at their leisure. So much for the plot. Now for the action.

It has always been my contention that Brigadier-General Herbert Firebrace rather brought it on himself. There are things which generals may do, and there are things which they may not; or shall we say, lest I be deemed guilty of *lèse majesté*, things it were better they did not? All things to them are lawful, but all things most undoubtedly are not expedient. And no one – not even his most fervent admirer – could say that the General's action was a wise one. Let it be understood that when the more exalted ones of the earth desire to make a tour of trenches, there is a recognised procedure for doing it. First comes the sergeant of the platoon occupying the portion of the line under inspection – experience has shown the wisdom of having the only trust-worthy guide in front. Then comes the company commander, followed by the Colonel, the Staff officer and the Great One. Immediately behind, the Adjutant (taking notes), the platoon commander (partially dazed), the machine-gun officer (not essential), and the Sapper (if he's been caught by the human avalanche) advance in echelon. At intervals the procession halts, and the same religious rite takes place.

SERGEANT (*peering round the next traverse, in voice of fury*): "Don't drink tea out of yer tin 'at, yer perisher! 'Ere's the General a-coming."

COLONEL (*prompted by the company commander*): "Now from here, sir, we get a most magnificent field of fire behind – ah – those craters there. I thought that – where was it we decided? – oh, yes, by – ah – putting a Lewis gun here...er, well, perhaps you'd like to see yourself, sir."

GREAT ONE: "Yes, very much. Have you got my peri-scope?" (*Staff officer produces, and Great One peers through it.*) "I quite agree with you." (*After long inspection*) "You might make a note of it."

STAFF OFFICER: "Just make a note of that, will you?"

ADJUTANT (*makes note*): "Make a note of it, Bill, will you?"

PLATOON COMMANDER (*recovering slightly from stupor*): "Make a note of what?"

MACHINE-GUN OFFICER: "All right, old boy. It's my pidgeon." (*Sotto voce to* SAPPER) "I've had a gun there for the last two nights." (*Aloud to* OMNES) "An excellent place, sir. I'll see to it."

SAPPER (*to* MGO, *with seeming irrelevance*): "Well, when he got to the house he was told she was having a bath, and – " Procession moves on, while infuriated sentry on sap duty misses the point of the story. And that is the right way of touring the trenches.

Unfortunately General Firebrace was a new broom. It was quite permissible for him to do what he did, but, as I said before, I am doubtful if it was altogether wise. In a moment of rashness he decided to go round the trenches alone. As a matter of fact, at the moment of this resolve the Brigade-Major was out, the evening was fine, and the General was energetic. Perfect peace reigned over that portion of the battle area which concerned him, and he was anxious to see that the arrangement of sentry groups in the various sap-heads met with his approval. His predecessor, he recalled, had had words with the still greater ones of the earth anent a couple of small, but nevertheless regrettable, incidents when men had been removed somewhat forcibly by the wily Hun from out those same sap-heads. So he settled his steel helmet firmly on his head, and stepped out of his dug-out into the communication trench.

Now in that particular part of the line the communication trenches were long ones, and by the time he reached the front line it was getting dark. A man of small stature, but withal fiery appearance, General Herbert Firebrace strode along through the deepening gloom, humming gently to himself. At first the trenches were fairly populous – he was in a part of the front line between two groups of craters – and he found it necessary to bark "Gangway!" continuously. Then he reached his goal, the saps behind one of the groups – short trenches which stretch out from the fire trench into No Man's Land and finish on the near lips of the craters. He grunted with satisfaction as he found the first of the saps held to his satisfaction. The sentry group were quietly smoking; the sentry up at the head of the sap was watching fixedly through his periscope. The rifles and bayonets of the men rested close at hand, the Mills bombs were conveniently placed on a narrow ledge under cover.

"Ha, good! All quiet here, my lads?"

"All quiet, sir," answered the corporal, scrambling up.

"That's all right. Good night, corporal." And the martial little figure disappeared round the corner.

Now the corporal was new in that bit of the line; to be exact, he had just returned from leave. That was one cause.

"Look out – oil-can!" The sentry gave a hail, and every one ducked. That was the other cause.

For at the precise moment that an oil-can exploded with a thunderous crump twenty yards or so beyond the trench, there was a sudden noise of ripping canvas, an agonised shout, and the heavy crash of a body encountering china. Then – silence. The sap parties heard only the oil-can; Percy FitzPercy for a wonder was not brooding over his invention, and there was no one who knew that close beside them in an odoriferous underground abode the Brigadier-General lay completely stunned, with his head in a metal soup tureen and his rather extensive set of uppers in a disused tin hitherto devoted to that painstaking gentleman, Mr Maconochie.

Up to this point it will be willingly conceded, I think, by anyone acquainted with trench etiquette that the unfortunate predicament of Herbert Firebrace, General and Great One, was only what he deserved. To depart so flagrantly from the spirit of the rules as to wander round front-line trenches alone and in the falling shades of night is asking for trouble; and if the matter had ended there I have no doubt – knowing the strict sense of justice which is one of the praiseworthy features of the house of Firebrace – I have no doubt that he would have sent for Percy FitzPercy and apologised handsomely for the inconvenience he had so unwittingly caused. But the matter did not end there; it only began. And the finale, reviewed dispassionately, undoubtedly gives one to think – one might even say think furiously.

A quarter of an hour after the regrettable occurrence just described Percy stood chatting lightly and inconsequently with his company commander in the support line. At the moment he was expatiating on the merits of a new pipe of his own invention designed for use in No Man's Land on a dark night. Its exact beauties escape my memory; as far as I can remember one put the bowl in one's mouth and the tobacco in the stem and blew. It was an invention typical of Percy – utterly futile. He had just called the company commander "dear old soul" for the tenth time, and was explaining how no sparks or glowing ash could be seen if you made use of this patent atrocity, when a Lewis gun started rattling away in front. Half a dozen Verey lights shot up, there was a sudden brisk burst of firing, with the explosion of a number of bombs.

"By Jove!" cried Percy, pipe and all else forgotten. "By Jove, dear old man – a raid – what? A Hun raid – now for the man-trap!" He departed at speed up the nearest boyau, leaving a trail of sparks behind him like a catherine-wheel that has been out in the rain; to be followed by his Captain, who had first taken the precaution of loading his automatic.

The first man Percy met was the tooth-sucker, who was shaking with uncontrollable excitement.

"There's a perisher fell in the 'ole, sir! Three of 'em come in, and we killed two an' the other fell in the 'ole."

I am given to understand that on receipt of the news what little intellect our pipe-inventor ever possessed completely deserted him. Uttering hoarse cries, he dashed down the trench, and, unmindful of his own orders to wait on the chance of catching a second, he feverishly slashed at the string, and with an ominous clang and a squelch of mud the trapdoor descended into its appointed position. Certain it is, when the company commander came in sight, he was standing upon it, in an attitude strongly reminiscent of the heavy tragedian – out of a "shop" – holding forth in his favourite Bodega.

"What the blazes are you doing there?" howled his infuriated Captain. "Why aren't you in number eight sap, instead of doing a dumb-crambo show?"

"The raid is over, sir," answered Percy majestically. "The raider is – ah – below."

"What the – " began the frenzied senior. And then he paused. "Great Scott! What's that infernal shindy?"

From below their feet there rose a perfect orgy of breaking china and rattling tins, with ever and anon a loud musical note as of a bucket being belaboured with a stick. Grunts and guttural curses, followed by strange hollow noises indicative of pain, for a while drowned all attempts at conversation. Finally there was a grand finale of crashing cups and tinkling tins, the sound of a heavy blow, a grunt of muffled agony and – silence. The lights still hissed up into the night, stray rifles still cracked at intervals, but otherwise – silence.

At last Percy spoke. "Do you know, dear old boy, I believe there are two of them down there; 'pon my soul, I do – what?" He spoke with deliberation, as befits an inventor. "It seemed to me that the one who swore and the one who grunted were different people."

The tooth-sucker opined likewise; also Tomkins, who had arrived on the scene.

"What is this dam' foolishness?" said the Captain irritably. "Am I to understand there are two Germans inside there, under the trench?"

"One for certain; two possibly – or even three, dear old boy." At the thought of three, he of the teeth played a tune in his excitement.

"Then for heaven's sake get the top off and let's get them out!"

It was then that the last cruel blow of Fate was dealt to the hapless Herbert. For after a brief period of feverish pulling, during which the company commander broke his nails and Percy fell over backwards, the trapdoor remained *in statu quo*.

"What the devil's the matter with the beastly thing?" muttered the Captain savagely. "It's your fool-trick, FitzPercy! Can't you open it?"

"My dear old boy," remarked the proud inventor vaguely, "it generally opens – 'pon my soul, it does." He turned his torch on to the reluctant trench-board and examined it through his eyeglass. "By Jove! that's it, dear old son, there's the trouble. The dud shell has slipped forward and got wedged in the rafters. How doocid funny – what?"

"What is doocid funny, you blithering ass?"

"Why, if we'd gone on, dear old sport, the shell might have gone off. By Jove, that's good, that is!" Percy chuckled immoderately. "If we go on, the shell goes off!"

"You're the type of man who ought to be in a home," remarked his senior officer dispassionately. "Get a saw as soon as you can, and cut through the board. And if the bally shell goes off and kills you, it'll serve you right. You're a disease, FitzPercy, that's what you are. A walking microbe; an example of atavism; a throw-back to the tail period." Still muttering, his company commander passed out of sight, leaving the triumphant Percy completely unabashed and glowing in righteous success.

Now, in the trenches saws do not grow freely. You cannot wander round a corner and pick one up; in fact, a saw that will saw is an exceeding precious thing. Moreover, they are closely guarded by their rightful owners, who show great reluctance in parting with them. It therefore was not surprising that over an hour elapsed before a perspiring messenger returned with one and operations commenced. And during that hour Percy lived.

It is given to few to see their hopes and aspirations realised so beautifully and quickly; as in a dream he listened to the hideous cachinnations that floated up through the slabs of the trench-board. A continuous booming noise as of a bittern calling to its young was varied with heavy grunts and occasional blows of a heavy bludgeon on metal. And throughout it all there ran a delicate *motif* of crashing cups and tinkling tins.

"We have them, dear old soul," murmured Percy ecstatically to himself; "we have them simply wallowing in the mulliga-tawny!"

But there is an end of everything – even of getting a saw out of an RE store. A glorious full moon shone down upon the scene as, an hour afterwards, the trench-board was removed and the entrance opened. An "up-and-over" – or trench-ladder – was lowered into the dug-out, and the excited onlookers waited to net the catch. At last the ladder shook, as the first of the prisoners prepared to ascend.

"Entrance, dear old man," cried the stage manager majestically, "of what we have hitherto described as 'male voices off.'"

"Get up, you swine, and get a move on!" rasped a voice in perfect English from the depths of the hole; while a palsied silence settled on the audience.

The ladder shook again, and at last there emerged from the bottom of the trench a large round tin which completely encased the head of its wearer, who followed slowly, maintaining a continuous booming roar. Immediately behind him came the owner of the voice, severely chipped about the face, but with the light of battle in his eyes.

"Now, you – " The words died away in his mouth. "Great heavens! The General!" And as the frozen eye of the speaker, who had been the other occupant of the hole, wandered round the stricken onlookers, even Percy's nerve broke. It was the Colonel.

I will draw the veil of reticence over the remainder of this harrowing narrative. The procession back to Brigade Head-quarters has become historic. The attempt to remove the soup tureen on the spot caused its unhappy possessor such agony, and gave rise to so much unseemly and ill-repressed mirth on the part of the audience, that it was hastily abandoned, and the wretched man was led gently back to his dug-out.

The Brigade-Major, who had been notified over the tele-phone, met him at the entrance with a handkerchief suspiciously near his mouth.

"How dreadful, sir!" he murmured, in a voice that shook a little. "I have – er – sent for a tin-opener."

The General was led to a chair, into which he sank wearily, while in hushed tones the Colonel explained what had happened to his shaking Staff.

"I was told that the General had been seen going down to the front line alone," he remarked in a low tone, "and so I at once followed him. Just as I got to the craters there was a small Hun raid. I let drive at one of them with my revolver, and the next instant I fell through a hole, full on top of someone's back. He let out a roar of pain and scrambled up. Of course I thought it was a Hun, and proceeded to beat him over the head with my stick. Great Scott, what a show!"

The Colonel mopped his brow, and the Staff shook still more.

"I'd dropped my revolver, or I'd probably have shot him. Then suddenly there was a clang, and the hole was closed up, while at the same moment something charged past me, head down, and hit the wall. There was a roar of pain, and the tin became a fixture. The poor old boy had rammed the wall with the soup tureen."

A gurgling noise from the chair interrupted him.

"What is it, sir?" cried the Staff Captain solicitously.

The General hooted mournfully.

"Yes, sir. He'll be here very soon, sir. Not much longer now. We've sent for a tinsmith from one of the Engineer companies."

But the booming cantata continued.

"What does he want?" whispered the Staff Captain. "A drink?"

The Brigade-Major looked hopeful.

"Yes; get a whisky and soda and a straw, if there's one left."

The booming died away.

A few minutes later the Staff, ably assisted by the General's batman, got one end of the straw into the worthy Brigadier's mouth. The Colonel closed those holes he could see with his fingers, and the signalling officer held the drink.

"Now, are we ready?" cried the Brigade-Major anxiously. "All right, sir – suck."

The experiment was not a success. Jets of liquid spurted in all directions, an explosion like a geyser shook the tin, and the Staff recoiled a pace. In fact, I am given to understand that the chief clerk, an intensely interested spectator, so far forgot himself as to counsel the Staff Captain to "sit on 'is 'ead."

"Do you think we could do anything with one of those instruments for opening tongues?" hazarded the Staff Captain, when the silence had become oppressive and the outbursts of fire extinguished.

"We might try." The signalling officer was doubtful, but sallied forth, and after some delay returned with one. "Where shall we start?"

"Any old place." The Staff Captain gripped the implement and stepped manfully forward. "We're going to try something else, sir – a tongue opener."

The General hooted apathetically; the onlookers looked anxious, and the Staff Captain got his first grip on the tin.

"Hold the General's head, Bill," he cried to the Brigade-Major, "so that I can get a purchase. Now, then – one – two – "

A howl of agony rent the air, and even the chief clerk looked pensive.

"It's his ear, you fool!" The Colonel dodged rapidly out of the door to evade the human tornado within, and the situation became crucial. Even the tinsmith, who arrived at that moment, a man of phlegmatic disposition, was moved out of his habitual calm and applauded loudly.

"Thank heavens you've come!" gasped the Brigade-Major, keeping a wary eye fixed on his frenzied senior, who, surrounded with debris and red ink, was now endeavouring to pull the tin off with his hands. "The General has had a slight mishap. Can you remove that tin from his head?"

The expert contemplated his victim in silence for a few moments.

"Yus," he remarked at length, "I can, sir, if 'e keeps quite still. But I won't be answerable for the consequences if 'e don't."

"No more will I." The Brigade-Major mopped his brow. "For heaven's sake get on with it."

Thus ended the episode of Percy FitzPercy – his man-trap.

It might have happened to anyone, but only FitzPercy would have searched carefully amongst the crockery, and having found what he was looking for made a point of bringing it to head-quarters just as the tin was finally removed.

To emerge into the light of two candles and an electric torch with a bit of one ear and half a face deficient, and realise that the man responsible for it is offering you your uppers in three parts and some fragments, is a situation too dreadful to contemplate.

As I said before, Percy gave up trying after about ten seconds.

CHAPTER 5

Ebeneezer the goat

Driver Robert Brown, as I have already remarked, was an admirable man in many ways. And I have frequently observed to other members of the mess, that one of the things that most endeared him to me was his love of animals.

Brown was not a beauty, I admit: his face was of the general-utility order, and he had a partiality for singing a dreadful song of which he only knew one line – at least that is all we ever heard, thank Heaven! At cockcrow, 'neath the midday sun, at eventide, did he foist upon a long-suffering world, with a powerful and somewhat flat voice, the following despairing wail: "What a faice, what a faice, what a norrible faice, lumme, what a faice she 'ad." Occasional streams of invective issued from neighbouring dug-outs. The result was immaterial; he merely appraised other portions of the lady's anatomy. Once I remember the cook was ill; Brown did his work. He was a good lad – he always did everyone else's work. We were hungry – very hungry – and he, stout fellow, was preparing our repast.

"Homlette, sir," he had murmured confidentially, "peas and taters, and fresh meat!" and with his honest face shining with eagerness to prepare this Epicurean banquet he had gone about his business. The shadows lengthened – an appetising smell greeted our nostrils; we forgave him his untoward references to his adored one's "faice." Then it happened.

"What a neye, what a neye, what a norrible neye, lumme" – there was a fearful pause and a sizzling noise – "lumme, the whole perishing homlette's in the fire." It was; and in a gallant attempt at rescue he upset the meat in an adjacent stagnant pool. The only thing we got were the peas, and they rattled on the tin plates like shrapnel bullets.

However, as I've said several times, he was an admirable lad, and a love of animals atoned for a multitude of sins. At least everyone thought so, until he adopted a goat. It was an animal of unprepossessing aspect and powerful smell – very powerful. I speak with some authority on the subject of goats, for in the course of my service I have lived for a space on an abominable island "set in a sapphire sea." Ninety per cent of its population are goats, the remainder priests; and without intermission, in a ceaseless stream, the savour of that island flows upwards and outwards. I therefore claim to speak with authority, and Brown's goat would have held its own with ease in any community.

He accommodated it in a special dug-out, from which it habitually escaped; generally at full speed just as the Major was passing. When the Major had been knocked down twice, Brown was accorded an interview. It was a breezy little affair, that interview, and Brown for some hours seemed a trifle dazed. For some time after he was busy in the goat's dug-out, and when I passed on my way out to a job of work that evening, I found him contemplating his handiwork with pride. Not content with doubling its head-rope, he had shackled the goat fore and aft to pegs in the ground – one fore-leg and one hind-leg being secured by rope to two pegs firmly driven into the floor of the dug-out.

"That's done you, my beauty," I heard him murmuring; and then he relapsed into his song, while the goat watched him pensively out of one eye.

I subsequently discovered that it was about three o'clock next morning it happened. The goat, having slipped its collar and pulled both pegs, shot from its dug-out with a goat-like cry of joy. Then the pegs alarmed it, dangling from its legs – and it went mad. At least, that's what the Major said. It appeared that, having conducted an exhaustive survey of a portion of the line with the General and his staff, they had returned to refresh weary nature with a portion of tongue and a bottle of fine old port – the old and bold, full of crustiness. Hardly had they got down to it, when, with a dreadful and ear-splitting noise, the goat bounded through the door of the dug-out. One peg flying round caught the General on the knee, the other wrapped itself round the leg of the table. The old gentleman, under the impression that the Germans had broken through, drew his revolver, and with a great cry of "Death rather than dishonour," discharged his weapon six times into the blue. Mercifully there were no casualties, as the staff, with great presence of mind, had hurled themselves flat on their faces during this dangerous proceeding. Each shot came to rest in the crate containing the whisky, and the fumes from the liquid which flowed over the floor so excited the goat that with one awful effort it broke loose and disappeared into an adjacent cornfield. I cannot vouch for all this – in fact the mess as a body received the story coldly. The junior subaltern even went so far as to murmur to another graceless youth that it was one way of accounting for eight bottles of whisky and two of port – and that it was very creditable to all concerned that they said it was a goat, and not a spotted megothaurus. All I can vouch for is that when the Major woke up the next day, he issued an ultimatum. The goat must go – alive if possible; dead if necessary – but if he ever again saw the accursed beast, he, personally, would destroy it with gun-cotton. As he really seemed in earnest about the matter, I decided that something must be done. I sent for Brown.

"Brown," I said when he appeared, "the goat must go."

"What, Hebeneezer, sir?" he answered in dismay.

"I do not know its name," I returned firmly, "and I was under the impression that it was a female; but if you call it Ebeneezer, then Ebeneezer must go." He became pensive. "Dead or alive that accursed mammal must depart, never to return. It has already seriously injured the Major's constitution."

"It has, sir?" There was a world of surprise in his tone. "Of course, it don't do to go playing about with it, or crossing it like, but – "

"The goat has done the crossing. Twice – at full speed."

" 'E seems a bit quiet this morning, sir. Off his food like. And 'e's lost a bit of 'is tail." Brown scratched his head meditatively.

The fact did not surprise me – but I preserved a discreet silence. "Get rid of it this morning, and see that it never returns!" I ordered, and the incident closed – at least I thought so at the time.

Brown reported his departure that evening, and with a sigh of relief from the Major the odoriferous Ebeneezer was struck off the strength with effect from that day's date. It is true that I noticed strange and mysterious absences on the part of my servant when he left carrying something in paper and returned empty-handed, and that in the back of my mind I had a vague suspicion that somewhere in the neighbourhood there still remained that evil-smelling animal looked after and fed by Robert Brown. But, as a week passed and we saw and smelt the beast no more, my suspicions were lulled to rest, and I dismissed the untoward incident from my mind. I am always of an optimistic disposition!

I should say it was about ten days after Ebeneezer's departure that I awoke one morning early to the sound of a violent altercation without.

"I tells you, you can't see the Major. 'E's in 'is bath." Peering out, I saw Brown and the cook warding off two extremely excited Belgians.

"Bath! Bath! *Qu'est que c'est* – bath!" The stouter Belgian gesticulated freely. "You are – vot you say – *du génie, n'est-ce-*

pas? Eet is important – ver important that I see monsieur le commandant."

"Look here, cully," murmured the cook, removing a clay pipe from his mouth and expectorating with great accuracy; "moosoo le commondant is in 'is bath – see. You'll 'ave to wait. Bath – savez. Eau." He pointed to a bucket of water.

"*Mon Dieu!*" shuddered the Belgian. "*Eh bien! mon ami*, ees zere anozer officer? It is *très important*." He was getting excited again. "*Les Boches* – zere is a *bruit* under ze earth – *comprenez?* Zey make a – oh! ze word, ze word – zey make *une mine*, and zen we all go Pouff!" He waved his hands to Heaven.

"Mean. Mean," remarked the cook contemplatively. "Wot the deuce does he mean? Anyway, Bob, we might take 'im on as a sparklet machine."

Then I thought it was about time I came to the rescue. "What's all the trouble, Brown?" I asked, coming out of the dug-out.

"These 'ere blokes, sir..." he began; but as both Belgians began talking at once, he got no further.

"Ah! monsieur," they cried, "*vous étes du génie?*" I assured them I was of the engineers. "Then come *vite, s'il vous plait*. We are of ze artillery, and ze Germans zey make *une mine, n'est-ce-pas?* We go up Pouff. Our guns zey go up Pouff – *aussi*."

"Mining," I cried, "the Germans mining here! Impossible, messieurs. Why, we're a mile and a half behind the firing-line." I regret to say I was a little peevish.

Nevertheless they assured me it was so – not once, but many times. Strange noises, they affirmed, were heard in the bowels of the earth near their battery – mysterious rumblings occurred; they continually assured me they were going Pouff!

I went to the Major. He was not in a good temper – he rarely is in the early morning – and the last blade of his safety razor was blunt.

"Mining here!" he barked. "What the deuce are they talking about? It's probably nesting time for woodpeckers or something. Oh! yes – go away and see," in reply to my question. "Anything to get those two embryo volcanoes off the premises: and don't let 'em come back, for Heaven's sake!"

So I went. Undoubtedly there were noises – very strange subterranean noises, in front of that battery. Moreover, the sounds seemed to come from different places. At times they were very loud; at others they ceased. The excitement soon became intense. Stout officers lay all over the ground with their ears pressed in the mud. The commandant of the battery ran round in small circles saying Pouff! distractedly. In fact everyone said Pouff! to everyone else. It became the password of the morning. Then at last the crucial moment arrived. The centre of the storm, so to speak, had been located – the place where, so far as we could tell, the noise seemed consistently loudest. At that point the Belgians started to dig; and instantly a triumphant shout rent the air. The place was an old disused shaft, boarded over and covered with a thin layer of earth. At last it was open, and from it there issued loud and clear a dreadful tapping.

"A network of galleries," cried an interpreter excitedly. "Probably old shafts reaching the German lines. We are lost." He and the commandant had a pouffing match in their despair. But now the noise became greater, and we heard distinctly a human voice. It was at that moment the dread suspicion first dawned on me. An army of men hung over the edge, armed to the teeth with pistols and bowie knives, tin cans and bits of brick. Tap, tap, louder and louder, came the noise. The Pouffers were silent – every one breathed hard.

Then suddenly I heard it echoing along the hollow gallery: "What a faice, what a faice, what a norrible faice – Hebeneezer, you perisher; where the 'ell are you? – lumme, what a faice she 'ad."

" 'The Watch on the Rhine.' They sing their accursed song," howled the commandant. "Belgium for ever, *mes braves!*"

It was at that moment that a stout spectator, moved to frenzy by this appeal, or else owing to a rush of blood to the head, hurled his tin can. Every one fired – a ghastly noise rent the gloom of the well; there was the sound of something departing at a great rate; a heavy fall; and then silence.

I walked thoughtfully back to my dug-out, refusing the offer of making further explorations. As I passed inside I met Brown. He was limping, and the skin was off his nose.

"What have you been doing?" I demanded.

"I fell down, sir," he answered.

"Brown," I said sternly, "where is the goat, Ebeneezer?"

Brown rubbed his nose and looked thoughtfully at me. "Well, sir, I can't say as 'ow I rightly know. 'E *was –* " Further disclosures were nipped in the bud by the sudden appearance of the Major. He was inarticulate with rage.

"Get me my revolver," he spluttered. "Get me my revolver. That damn' goat's come back and knocked me down again!"

But Brown had discreetly vanished.

CHAPTER 6

The pepnotised milk

Aunt Araminta is one of the dearest souls that ever breathed. I may say at once that she is not my aunt – rather does she belong to a subaltern of the unit. But we all feel a sort of proprietary right to Aunt Araminta. In the past she has supplied us all with many things. During the winter we received frequent consignments of cholera belts and socks, gloves and khaki handkerchiefs. Most of them had moth balls sewn in. I have never seen her, but I unhesitatingly state that she is of the moth-ball type – she is a martyr to them. This conclusion is confirmed by her nephew – a graceless youth. Now I regret to say that much of our affection for the elderly Araminta has gone. It may return in time – but she has been directly responsible for our being sent to the front-line trenches when we were enjoying a comparative rest on a somewhat safer line. No doubt she was actuated by the best intentions in the world, but just at present we don't mention her if the Major is about.

It all occurred owing to a shortage of milk – condensed or otherwise. We were on a line, which though safe – or more or less so – did not admit of our obtaining the genuine article with any ease. I appealed to Driver Robert Brown, our sheet-anchor – our Admirable Crichton. He it is who buys us eggs; he gets us bread and pork chops; anon he obtains tinned salmon mingled with sardines. Once he essayed some fizzy water – Eau Gazeuse is, I believe, the correct name. Something got mixed, and the mess lowered a dozen Apenta before retiring to bed. However, that is another story.

Into the ears then of this our guide and mentor, our home within a home, our ever-ready gas cooker, I whispered the word milk. He said he knew of a cow, and he'd see what could be done.

Soon after he left with a tin receptacle and an air of determination; an hour after he returned with neither. He retired into the cook-house, and shortly after there came voices in wordy warfare.

"You mean to say you ain't got no milk?" demanded the cook aggrievedly.

"No – I ain't." Brown emerged and mopped his brow wearily.

"Couldn't you find the cow? I told you where it was." The Doctor's orderly ceased placing chloride of lime on the tomb of a rat. "And wot *'ave* you done to your face? It's 'orrible. Worse than usual."

"Less about my face." Brown's retort was a trifle heated. "I tells you, when I got to that there place you told me of – you couldn't see the perishing cow for the crowd. There was a row of blokes with mess tins, and one of 'em 'ad a dixie. When it come to my turn, I sits down by the old girl, and puts the tin on the floor. I got one jet going for about five seconds and that missed the blooming bucket. Then she shut up, and not another drop could I get. A perisher in the gunners, 'e says, 'Pull 'arder' 'e says, 'Great strength returns the penny.' So I got down to it like, just to wake 'er up, when blowed if she didn't 'op it. 'Opped it, and kicked me in the faice as a souvenir." He felt the injured member tenderly.

"I don't know as 'ow I notice much the matter with it." The cook gazed impassively at Brown's face. "It looks just like it always did, worse luck. But then it ain't the sort of face as is affected by little things like that. As the medical profession observed it is a norrible thing – your face. Ain't it, Bob?"

This appeal for confirmation to the face's owner touched me greatly. However, as I am quite unable to record the answer – and the rest of the conversation does not call for comment – I will pass on to the moment when I mentioned the shortage of condensed milk and the failure up to the present to supply the genuine to an indignant mess. I may mention – *en passant* – that in a moment of imbecility I had permitted myself to be thrust into the position of mess caterer. The Doctor used to do it – but he fell in love, and was unable to do anything but play "Somewhere a Voice is Calling" on the gramophone. As the record was cracked, there was a general feeling of relief when the junior subaltern strafed a mouse with it. However, the Doctor being beyond human help, his mantle descended on me. I was away when it did so – but that is by the way. The result would probably have been the same. Brown, as I have said, did it all; but I was the figurehead – on me descended the wrath of outraged officers compelled to eat sardines past their first youth, and the scene after the little episode of the Apenta water was quite dreadful.

"Why not go yourself and milk the bally cow if Brown can't?" remarked one of them unfeelingly. "Sing to it, dearie – one of those little ballads of your early youth. Something is bound to occur."

And then up spake Horatius – it *is* his name – he being the one that owned Aunt Araminta. "The old girl has just written me asking me if we want anything. I'll tell her to send some condensed along. Of course it won't be here for some time – but it's better than nothing." He turned over the last sheet. "She is sending a hamper, as a matter of fact. Perhaps there'll be some in it."

"Two to one it's nothing but moth balls," remarked the Doctor irreverently. "Heavens! do you remember the time the old dear got one mixed up in her home-made potted meat – and the Major broke his tooth on it."

It was the next day that the parcel arrived. A shower of white balls descended to the floor, two odd socks, some peppermint bull's-eyes, a letter, and *the* bottle.

"Great heavens!" muttered Horatius, gingerly inspecting the collection. "What has the old girl sent?" He opened the letter, read it, and asked for whisky.

MY DEAR NEPHEW – *he read, in a hushed voice.* I am sending you a bottle of the new milk – Dr Trapheim's Pepnotised Milk. As you will gather from perusing the label on the bottle, it is a marvellous discovery. At first I feared from the inventor's name that he might be of Germanic extraction, but subsequent inquiries enabled me to discover that he is in reality the son of a Swedish Jew who married a girl from Salt Lake City. So, of course, he must be all right.

In this wonderful milk, my dear nephew, there are three million germs to the cubic foot – or is it inch? I forget which. Anyway, a very large number of nutritious germs exist in it. You remember poor Pluto?

"The pug," he explained hoarsely, and continued reading.

Regularly for a week before his death he drank a saucerful each night – and it eased him wonderfully. You remember his dreadful asthma. It quite left him, and he would lie for hours without movement after drinking it.

I hastened to buy a bottle – and send it to you all, with my very best wishes,

Your affectionate,

AUNT ARAMINTA.

PS – It may have different effects on different people. The cook, silly girl, has given notice.

And for a space there was silence. Then Horatius picked up the bottle, and in a hushed voice recited the label.

"Cures consumption, eradicates eczema, intimidates itch, and routs rabies. Makes bonny bouncing babies." He choked slightly, and passed it on to me. There was nothing that milk wouldn't do. Its effect on the human system was like rare wine, only permanent. It caused a clarity of vision, an improvement in intellect, a brightening of brain that started with the first bottle drank, and increased and multiplied with every succeeding bottle. It enlarged the bust in one paragraph, and removed double chins in another. Old and young alike thrived on it – it was the world's masterpiece in health-giving foods. Moreover it was impossible to tell it from ordinary milk when drinking it. That was its great charm. It could be used in tea or coffee or drunk neat. It made no odds. After one sip you bagged a winner. The betting was about a flyer to a dried banana skin that after a bottle you became a sort of superman.

It was while we were sitting a little dazedly with the bottle occupying a position of honour in the centre of the dug-out that we heard the Major's voice outside – also the General's, to say nothing to two staff officers. They had walked far and fast, and I gathered from the conversation that *Percy the pip-squeak* – gun, small, Hun variety – had thrust himself upon them. Their tempers did not seem all that one could desire. The prevalent idea, moreover, appeared to be tea.

"We'd better decant it, in a jar," said Horatius gloomily. "The General loathes tea without milk, and it says on the bottle you can't tell the difference."

The Doctor, however, was firm. He refused to allow anyone to drink it without being told, and as he pointed out if you tell a distinctly warm and irritable old gentleman that the apparently harmless liquid he sees in an ordinary jug on the table is in reality a pepnotised breed with three million germs to the cubic inch in it – he will probably not be amused, but will send you back to the trenches as a dangerous individual.

Horatius pointed out still more gloomily that to offer the old gentleman a bottle which expressly set out to eradicate eczema and intimidate itch was an even less likely way to his favour.

The General's entrance at that moment, however, settled the matter, and we began tea. It was not a cheerful meal to start with – rather the reverse. In fact, when I had explained and apologised for the absence of any milk, and introduced the bottle to the meeting, the atmosphere of the dug-out resembled a lawyer's office when the relatives hear their aunt's money has been left to a society for providing cannibals with unshrinkable wool underclothes.

"Who sent the damn' stuff?" asked the Major coldly.

"Aunt Araminta." Horatius nervously removed the wire that held in the cork. One of the staff officers carefully picked up the bottle and proceeded to read the label, while the General's expression was that of a man who gazes at short range into the mouth of a gun.

"It's wonderful stuff," continued Horatius. "Roll, bowl, or pitch, you bag a coconut every time you drink it. My aunt, sir, speaks most highly of it." He turned to the General, who received the news without enthusiasm.

"Three million bugs to the cubic inch," read the staff officer musingly. "And if there are twenty cubic inches in the bottle, we get sixty million bugs. Allowing for casualties, and in order to be on the safe side in case the makers swindled, call it fifty million."

"I think," remarked the General, breaking an oppressive silence, "I will have a whisky and soda."

It was at that moment I noticed the cork. My shout of warning came too late. With great force and a noise like a black Maria, it flew from the bottle, and from point-blank range embedded itself in the General's left eye. The entire mess became covered with a species of white foam, but the General took the

84

brunt. For a moment there was a dreadful silence, and then with a wild shout we hurled ourselves through the doorway. I have smelt many smells in many cities: I have stood outside tallow works. I have lived in the salient of Ypres. I have – but why elaborate? I say it with solemnity and earnestness: I have never smelt anything like that milk? Never in my wildest moments have I imagined that such a smell could exist. It was superhuman, stupendous, wonderful.

The General, who had lost his eyeglass in the excitement and then trodden on it, was running round in small circles, holding his nose. He was unable at any time to see with his right eye, and a portion of cork still remained in his left. Without cessation he trumpeted for assistance.

"Wipe it off," he howled. "Wipe the damn' stuff off, you fat-headed idiots." He fell heavily into a Johnson hole, and became temporarily winded.

From all directions men were emerging with helmets on, thinking a new form of gas had been evolved by the Hun. A neighbouring doctor, seeing the General in a recumbent position, rushed up to render assistance, while two staff officers, assisted by the Major, made gingerly dabs at the old gentleman with handkerchiefs.

At last it was over. The cork plucked from his eye, he arose and in splendid isolation confronted us. After swallowing hard once or twice, he spoke.

"I do not know if this was a jest." His voice was hoarse. "My eyeglass is broken, the sight of my other eye irreparably damaged. I am now going to Corps Headquarters, and provided the Corps Commander can sit in the same room with that cursed woman's fifty million stinking bacilli, I propose to ask him to let you try them at once on the Germans."

Amidst a solemn hush he departed – with two staff officers at a discreet distance. I gather that the spectacle of their departure by car, with the one who'd failed to get the seat next to the driver sitting on the step at the side, and the General enthroned alone like a powerful-smelling fungoidal growth, was not the least pathetic incident of the afternoon.

But Aunt A is not popular.

CHAPTER 7

Driver Robert Brown

Four or five years ago, in the dim, hazy time when Europe lay at peace, there arrived at the station in England where I was fortunate enough to be serving a batch of eight recruits. They were very raw and very untrained, and it was the doubtful pleasure of the unit in which I was, to undertake periodically the training of such batches in order to relieve a somewhat overtaxed depot elsewhere. This batch – like unto other similar batches – aspired to become drivers in His Majesty's Corps of Royal Engineers. Occasionally their aspirations were realised – more often not, for the terms of their service were two years with the colours and ten with the reserve, and at the end of two years the average man may just about be considered capable of looking after two horses and a set of harness – really looking after them – and not before. Then they go, or most of them, and the service knows them no more. However, all that is beside the point.

Wandering dispassionately round the stables one day, I perceived the eight, mounted on blankets, sitting on their horses, while a satirical and somewhat livery rough-riding corporal commented on the defects of their figures, their general appearance, and their doubtful claim to existence at all, in a way that is not uncommon with rough-riders. Then for the first time I saw Brown – Driver Robert Brown, to give him his full name.

"I 'ad a harnt once, No. 3. She was sixty-four, and weighed twenty stone. And if she'd 'a been sitting on that there 'orse of yours she'd have looked just like you: only 'er chest grew in front and not be'ind like yours."

No. 3 was Driver Robert Brown. I passed on. The presence of an officer sometimes tends to check the airy persiflage which flows so gracefully from the lips of riding instructors.

A week after I inquired of the corporal as to the progress of his charges. "Not bad, sir," he said – "not bad. The best of them easy is that there Brown. He don't look much on a horse – in fact, he looks like a sack o' potatoes – but 'e's a tryer, and we'll turn 'im into something before we've done."

Then one day – about four in the afternoon – I happened to wander through the stables. They were deserted apparently save for the stableman – until, in a corner, I came upon Driver Brown. He was giving his horse sugar, and making much of him – to use the riding-school phrase. We had a talk, and he told me things, when he got over his shyness – about his parents and where he lived, and that he loved animals, and a lot else besides. From then on I kept my eye on Brown, and the more I did so, the more I liked him. He was no beauty – he was not particularly smart – but he was one of the best. His NCOs swore by him – his two horses had never looked better – his harness was spotless. In addition to that he played back in the football eleven, if not with great skill, at any rate with immense keenness. He had exactly the figure for a zealous full back, and was of the type who kicked with such vim that when he missed the ball – which he generally did – he invariably fell heavily to the ground. Thus Robert Brown – recruit.

When his two years were up, Brown elected to stay on in the service. The service consisting in this case of his commanding officer, his NCOs and myself, it could find no reason why he shouldn't – in fact, and on the contrary, many very excellent reasons why he should. So Brown took on for his seven. Shortly afterwards, owing to a marked propensity of my servant to combine the delights of old Scotch with the reprehensible custom of sleeping off those delights in my best easy chair – one bought on the hire system, not the Government issue, where sleep under any circumstances is completely out of the question – owing, as I say, to this unpleasant propensity, I approached my commanding officer. NCOs were annoyed – they entreated, they implored, and the issue was in doubt, till a providential attack of influenza laid my CO low for the time, and the senior subaltern – myself – reigned in his stead. Then the sergeant-major laughed, and resigned himself to the inevitable. Driver Robert Brown became my servant, and the desecrator of my padded armchair retired – after a short period of durance vile – to seek repose on stable buckets.

During the forthcoming six months I am bound to admit I suffered – dreadfully. You do not make a servant in a day; but he tried his level best. We had shirt parades, in which I instructed him in the art of studding shirts, with little hints thrown in as to the advisability of wreaking his will on the shirt for dinner before he cleaned my parade boots for the following morning – not after. We delved into the intricacies of washing lists, and he waxed indignant over the prices charged. They seemed to me quite ordinary, but Brown would have none of it. I did not often study them – bills were never one of my hobbies; but one day it suddenly struck me the month's bill was smaller than usual. That was the awful occasion when changing quickly for cricket. I thought something was wrong with the shirt; it seemed rather stiffer in front than the average flannel – moreover, it had no buttons. Howls for Brown. Vituperation for lack of buttons.

"But, sir, that's an evening shirt you've got on. One I washed myself to save the washing bill." Tableau.

Then I prepared lists on pieces of paper as to the exact things I required packed in my suitcase when I departed for weekends.

There was the hunting weekend, and the ball-dance weekend, and the weekend when I stayed 'neath the parental roof, and – er – other weekends too numerous to mention. I would grunt Dance, or Home, or Brighton at him when he brought me my tea on Friday morning, and then during the morning he would, with the aid of the correct list, pack the necessary. There were occasional lapses. Once I remember – it was lunchtime on Friday, and we were being inspected. The mess was full of brass hats, and my train was 2.45. I had howled Dance at Brown as I passed my room before lunch, and was hoping for the best, when the mess waiter told me my servant wanted me for a moment. I went outside.

"Please, sir, them thin ones of yours is full of holes and the other three are at the wash." His voice like himself was good and big. "Shall I run down and buy a pair and meet you at the station?"

All the general said when I returned was, "Did he mean socks?"

Then there was a dreadful occasion when he sent me away one weekend with one of his dickies in my bag – he had been promoted to mufti – instead of a dress shirt; and another even more awful when he sent me to an austere household – prayers at eight, etc. – from the owner of which I had hopes, with my boots wrapped in a paper of orange hue which had better be nameless. I could continue indefinitely – the mistakes that lad made would have built a church; but withal I never wish for a better servant – a truer-hearted friend. And all this happened in the long dim ages way back before we started – he and I – with thousands of others for the land across the water; where for a space he remained my servant, until in the fullness of time he passed down that Long Valley from which there is no return. Many have passed down it these last months – many will pass down it before Finis is written on this World War; but none deserve a gentler crossing over the Great Divide than Robert Brown, Driver, RE, and sometime batman.

Now should there be any who, having read as far as this, hopefully continue in the belief that they are getting near the motto – in the shape of some wonderful deed of heroism and daring – they will, I am afraid, be disappointed. I have no startling pegs on which to hang the tale of his life. Like thousands of others, he never did anything very wonderful – he never did anything at all wonderful. He was just one of the big army of Browns out here of whom no one has ever heard. One of that big army who have done their bit unrewarded, unknown – because it was the thing to do; a feeling unknown to some of those at home – I allude to the genus Maidenhead Maggot still seen in large quantities – er – resting. And yet for each of those Browns – their death recorded so tersely in the paper – some heart-broken woman has sobbed through the long night, watching the paling dawn with tear-stained eyes, aching for the sound of footsteps for ever still, conjuring up again the last time she saw her man, now lying in a nameless grave. Would the Maggot get as much? I wonder.

As I have said, I'm afraid I haven't got anything very wonderful to describe. You can't make a deathless epic out of a man being sick – dreadfully sick beside the road – and an hour afterwards getting your food for you. It doesn't sound very romantic, I admit, and yet – It was in the morning, I remember, about three o'clock, that we first smelt it, and we were lying about half a mile behind the line. That first sweet smell of chlorine turning gradually into the gasping, throat-racking fumes. Respirators weren't regarded with the same importance then as they are now, but we all had them. Of course I'd lost mine. Since early childhood I have invariably lost everything. Brown found it, and I put it on – and then he disappeared. Some two hours later, when the shelling had abated a little, and the gas had long since passed, I found him again. He was white and sweating, and the gas was in him – not badly, you understand, not badly – but the gas was in him. For three or four hours he was sick, very sick – and his head was bursting. I know what he felt like.

And I said to the major, "I'm sorry it's Brown, but it'll teach him a lesson not to lose his respirator again," for, that is the way with Thomas Atkins – he is apt to lose most things that are not attached to him by chains.

It doesn't sound at all romantic all this, does it? – and yet, well, I found *my* respirator in the pocket of another coat. And as Brown came in with some food – he'd recovered about an hour – I handed him back *his* respirator, and I asked him why he'd done it.

"Well, I thought as 'ow you might 'ave to be giving orders like, and would want it more than me." He spoke quite naturally.

I didn't thank him – I couldn't have spoken to save my life – but the lad knew what I thought. There are some things for which thanks are an insult.

There was another thing which comes to me too, as I write – nothing very wonderful again, and yet – In the course of our wanderings we were engaged upon a job of work that caused us to make nightly a pilgrimage through Wipers. At the time Wipers was not healthy. That stage of the war of attrition – I understand that many of the great thinkers call it a war of attrition, though personally I wish they could be here when the Hun is attriting, or whatever the verb is – that stage, then, known as the second battle of Ypres was in progress. And, though all of that modern Pompeii was unhealthy at the time, there were certain marked places particularly so. One such was the Devil's Corner. There, nightly, a large number of things – men and horses – were killed; and the road was littered with – well, fragments.

Now it chanced one night that I had taken Brown with me to a point inside the salient, and at midnight I had sent him away – back to the field the other side of Ypres, where for the time we were lying. Two or three hours after I followed him, and my way led me past the Devil's Corner. All was quite quiet – the night's hate there was over, at any rate for the moment. One house was burning fiercely just at the corner, and the only sounds that broke the silence were the crackling of the flames and the occasional clatter of a limbered wagon travelling fast down a neighbouring road. And then suddenly I heard another sound – clear above my own footsteps. It was the voice of a man singing – at least, when I say singing – it was a noise of sorts. Also there was no mistaking the owner of the voice. Too often had I heard that same voice apostrophising "a beautiful picture, in a beautiful golden fraime." I stopped surprised – for what in the name of fortune Brown was doing in such an unsavoury spot was beyond me! In fact, I felt distinctly angry. The practice of remaining in needlessly dangerous places is not one to be encouraged. I traced that noise; it came from behind an overturned limber, with two defunct horses lying in the ditch. I crossed the road and peered over.

Sitting in the ditch was Robert Brown, and on his knees rested the head of the limber driver. In the breaking dawn you could see that the end was very near – the driver had driven for the last time. From the limp sag of his back I thought it was broken, and a bit of shell had removed – well, no matter, but one could hear the beating of the wings. Brown didn't see me, but occasionally, gentle as a woman, he bent over him and wiped the death sweat from his forehead; while all the time, under his breath, mechanically, he hummed his dirge. Then the man, lying half under the limber, stirred feebly.

"What is it, mate?" said Brown, leaning forward.

"Take the letters out of my pocket, matey," he muttered. "Them blokes at the War Office takes so long – and send 'em to – to – " The lips framed the words feebly, but no sound came.

"Who to, pal?" whispered Brown; but even as he spoke the poor maimed form quivered and lay still. And as I watched Brown lay his head gently down, and closed his eyes, the road, the houses seemed to grow a trifle misty. When I next looked up I saw him stumping away down the road, and, as he rounded the corner, a dreadful noise stating that, with regard to a lady named Thora, "he had loved 'er in life too little, 'e 'ad loved 'er in death too well," came floating back in the still air.

Yet methinks no great man's soul, speeded on its way by organ and anthem, ever had a nobler farewell than that limber driver, if the spirit of the singer has anything to do with it.

But, as I said before, I could continue indefinitely. Was there not the terrible occasion when I found him standing guard over a perfectly harmless Belgian interpreter, with a pick in his hand and the light of battle in his eye, under the impression that he had caught a German spy? The wretched man had lain on the ground for three hours – every movement being greeted with a growl of warning from Brown and a playful flourish of his pick. Also the awful moment when in an excess of zeal he built the Major a canvas chair, which collapsed immediately he sat in it, thereby condemning my irate commanding officer to walk in a bent-up position with the framework attached to his person, till his howls of rage produced deliverance. But time is short, and the pegs are small. He was just one of the Robert Browns, that's all; and the last peg in the lad's life is perhaps the smallest of all.

It was wet two or three days ago, very wet; and I, as usual, had gone out without a macintosh. We were away back west of Ypres, in a region generally considered safe. It is safe as a matter of fact by comparison, but occasionally the Hun treats us to an obus or two – lest we forget his existence. I got back very wet, very angry, and very bored, and howled for Brown. There was no answer, save only from the doctor's orderly, and he it was who told me. Brown had started out when the rain came on, six or seven hours before, with my macintosh, and, not returning, they had gone to look for him.

In a ditch they found him with the water dyed crimson, a few minutes before he died. It was just a stray shell that found its mark on the lad. I can see him in my mind stumping along the road, humming his song – and then, without warning, the sudden screech close on top of him, the pitiful, sagging knees, the glazing film of death, with none to aid him through as he had helped that other, for the road was little used.

Thank God! they found him before the end, but he only made one remark. "I couldn't get no farther, Dick," he muttered, "but the mack ain't stained."

I went up to see him in the brewery where they'd carried him, and I looked on his honest, ugly face for the last time. "The mack ain't stained." No, lad, it isn't. May I, when I come to the last fence, be able to say the same.

Though he spoke it literally, there is, methinks, a man's religion in those last words of Robert Brown, Driver, RE, and sometime batman.

CHAPTER 8

The end of "Wipers"

A nice balmy day, a good motor-car, and a first-class lunch in prospect. Such was my comparatively enviable state less than a month ago. True, the motor-car's springs had had six months' joy riding on the roads of Flanders, and the lunch was to be in Ypres; but one can't have everything – and Wipers was quite a pleasant spot then. In the square, souvenir hunters wandered through the Cloth Hall and the cathedral intent on strange remnants of metal for the curious at home. Tobacco shops did a roaring trade – market day was on. Villainous fragments of fried fish changed-hands for a consideration, and everyone was happy and contented.

Into a delightful little shop I ultimately found my way. Twelve small tables, spread with spotless linen, and, needless to say, full of officers satisfying the inner man, presided over by two charming French girls, seemed good enough for me, and, sure enough, the luncheon was on a par with the girls, which is saying "some" in the vernacular. As I left with a consignment of the most excellent white wine, for thirsty officers elsewhere, two soldiers passed me.

"Say, Bill," said one, "this 'ere Wipers is a bit of orl right. They can leave me here as long as they likes." And as I crossed the railway at the western end of the town, one shell passed sullenly overhead, the first I had heard that day – the only discordant note, the only sound of war. That was a month ago.

A fortnight ago duty took me past the same little shop and through the square. This time I did not linger – there were no souvenir hunters; there was no market day. Again I was in a motor-car, but this time I rushed through – hoping for the best. Instead of one shell they came in their hundreds. A drunken, swaying noise through the air, like a tramway-car going homewards on its last journey down an empty road, a crash and the roar of the explosion, mixed with the rumble of falling masonry. Another house gone in the dead city. Huge holes clawed up in the *pavé* road, and in every corner dead and twisted horses. Children lying torn in the gutter, women and men gaping in their death agony. Here and there a soldier; legs, arms, fragments of what were once living, breathing creatures. And in nearly every house, had one gone in, little groups of civilians still moaning and muttering feebly. They had crept into their homes, frightened, terrified – to wait for the death that must come. And without cessation came the shells. In one corner a motor-ambulance stood drunkenly on three wheels; in the middle a wagon overturned with four dead horses still fast in the traces, and underneath them stuck out two legs, the legs of what had been the lead driver. A city of the dead – not a sign of visible life, save only our car picking its way carefully through dead horses and masses of bricks fallen across the road. Yesterday's tobacco buyers stiff in the gutters; yesterday's vendors of fish dying in some corner like rats in a trap; yesterday's luncheon-shop a huge hole in the wall with the rafters twisted and broken, and the floor of the room above scattered over the twelve tables with the spotless linen. And perhaps – worst of all – the terrible, all-pervading stench which seemed to brood like a pall over everything.

At last we were clear of the square and getting into the open east of the town. Over the bridge and up a slight incline – then clear above the noise of the car for one most unpleasant second we heard the last tram going home. The next second a deafening roar, and we were in the centre of the stifling black fumes of a present from Krupps. All would have been well but for a dead horse in the centre of the road, which caused an abrupt stop. We left the car till the fumes had cleared away, and stumbled, gasping into the air, with the water pouring out of our eyes and the fumes catching our throats. And it was then we saw yesterday's Tommy who had regarded "Wipers" as a "bit of orl right."

Staggering down the road came three men, lurching from side to side, bumping up against one another, then falling apart: ever and anon collapsing in the road or the gutter, disappearing into shell holes, tripping over debris, over trees, over dead things. Gasping and panting they came on with their legs not strong enough to hold them. Nearer they came, and their faces were yellow-green, and their foreheads were thick with sweat, though the evening was chilly. They were half sobbing, half moaning, with their collars open and their clothes coated in mud. And one of them had a great gash over his head. Just before they reached us he collapsed in the ditch – for the last time. He was leaning forward and heaving with the agony of getting his breath. A froth was forming on his mouth, and his face was green.

"In God's name what is it?" we asked one of the other two as they staggered by. He stared at us vacantly, gasped out the one word, "Gas," and disappeared into the shambles of Ypres. We had not seen it before. We have since, and the first horror of it is past: but as there is a heaven above, there is not a man who has seen its effects who would not give every worldly possession he has to be able slowly to dribble the contents of a cylinder of the foulest and most diabolical invention yet conceived into a trench full of the originators of a device which most savages would be ashamed to use. We picked up the poor devil in the ditch and got him to a dressing station. He died in fearful agony half an hour after, so I subsequently heard. That was a fortnight ago.

Four nights ago there was a great light in the sky. Standing up out of the blaze, what was left of the cathedral showed up like a blackened sentinel. Through the trees the yellow flames shone with a lurid glow, and the crashing of falling houses completed the destruction started by German shells. The sight was one which will never be forgotten by those who saw it – that final gutting of a stricken town. For three days and three nights it blazed, and now all is over. It is the best end for that historic city – the scene of so much senseless carnage. How many of its harmless inhabitants have perished with it will never be known – will probably never be even guessed at. But fire is a purifier, and purification was necessary in Ypres.

CHAPTER 9

The black sheep

No one could have called Herbert Jones brilliant: his best friend – if he possessed such a thing – would not have predicted a great future for him. Into the manner of his living during the first twenty years of his life it would be well not to inquire too closely. Herbert Jones – more generally known to his inmates as 'Erb – was a dweller in dark places; one of the human flotsam who emerge like rats from their holes at night and spend in the nearest gin palace the few pence they have nefariously earned during the day. He was just a product of the gutter; from the gutter he came and to the gutter he returned in the fullness of time. And this was the way of it.

Personally I never made the acquaintance of Herbert Jones: such information as I possess of his disreputable history was told me one night at a dreary crossroads three or four miles east of Ypres, with the greenish flares lighting the sky all around us and the stench of dead horses in our nostrils. My informant was one of my drivers who had lived in the same street with him in London.

What it was that had caused a temporary ebullition of decent feeling in such an unpromising subject I was unable to find out. It was something to do with a lady called Lizzie Green, too much gin, and a picture palace which displayed a film of the Royal Horse Artillery galloping into action. In view of the fact that ninety per cent of Herbert's income was derived from making himself a public pest at jobbing stables, he quite naturally posed as a horsey youth, and that fact, coupled with Lizzie, the gin, and the film, apparently produced this one ebullition of decent feeling of which I have spoken. He enlisted. The very next day he presented his unprepossessing personality at a recruiting office – and his slum knew him no more. The Royal Regiment swallowed him up, gave him a uniform, decent food, and prepared to make a man of him.

It failed – hopelessly, dismally. The revilings of officers, the cursings of sergeants, the blasphemy of bombardiers alike failed to produce the slightest effect. His conduct sheet rapidly assumed the appearance of a full-sized novel; but there he was and there he remained – a driver in the Field Artillery, and the black sheep of his battery.

A year later found him at Havre. From there he drifted to Rouen – reviled by everyone who had the misfortune to have anything to do with him. At last, like a bad penny, he turned up again at his old battery, to the horror of all concerned, who thought they had effectually got rid of him at the beginning of the war. But the ways of record officers are wonderful – passing the ways of women. So when the news was broken to the major, and he had recovered, he ordered him to be put with the ammunition limbers, whose job it is to take ammunition to the battery nightly when they are in action and then return for more. And the captain, whose job is largely ammunition supply, heard his history from the sergeant whose job is entirely ammunition supply, and their remarks would be unprintable. Two nights later the battery was in action in the salient somewhere east of Ypres, and the reserves of ammunition were away back somewhere to the west, and Herbert Jones was with the reserves.

In the official *communiqués* it was known as a time of artillery activity in the neighbourhood of Ypres: in the *communiqués* of the battery it was known as a time of hell let loose; but especially was it so known among the ammunition limbers who nightly passed from west to east with full limbers and returned from east to west with empty ones. For, as may be seen by anyone who takes the trouble to procure an ordnance map, all roads from the west converge on Ypres, and having passed through the neck of the bottle diverge again to the east; which fact is not unknown to the Germans. So the limbers do not linger on the journey, but, at an interval of ten yards or so, they travel as fast as straining horseflesh and sweating drivers can make them. In many places a map is not necessary – even to a stranger. The road is clearly marked by what has been left at its side – the toll of previous journeys of limbers, who went out six in number and returned only four. And, should the stranger be blind, another of his senses will lead him unfailingly along the right road, for these derelict limbers and their horses have been there some time.

The Germans were searching the road leading to Ypres from the crossroads where I sat waiting for an infantry working party that had gone astray, on the first of the two occasions on which I saw 'Erb: that is to say, they were plastering a bit of the road with shells in the hope of bagging anything living on that bit. In the distance the rumble of wagons up the road was becoming louder every minute. All around us – for it was a salient – green flares lit up the sky, showing where the front trenches lay, and occasional rolls of musketry, swelling to a crescendo and then dying fitfully away, came at intervals from different parts of the line. A few spent bullets pinged viciously overhead, and almost without cessation came the angry roar of high-explosive shrapnel bursting along the road or over the desolate plough on each side. Close to me, at the crossroads itself, stood the remnants of a village – perhaps ten houses in all. The flares shone through the ruined walls – the place stank of death. Save for the noise it was a Dead World – a no-man's land. In the little village two motor-ambulances balanced themselves like drunken derelicts. Dead horses lay stiff and distended across the road, and a few over-turned wagons completed the scene of desolation.

Then, suddenly, over a slight rise swung the ammunition limbers – grunting, cursing, bumping into shell holes and out again. I watched them pass and swing away right-handed. In the rear came six pairs of horses, spare – in case. And as the last one went by a man beside me said, "Hallo! there's 'Erb." It was then I got his history.

An hour later I was back at that same place, having caught my wandering infantry party and placed them on a line with instructions to dig and continue digging till their arms dropped off. But when I got there I found it had changed a little in appearance, that dreary crossroads. Just opposite the bank where I had sat were two horses lying in the road and the legs of a man stuck out from underneath them, and they had not been there an hour before. The horses' heads were turned towards Ypres, and it seemed to me that there was something familiar in the markings of one of them.

With the help of my drivers we pulled out the man. It was no good – but one never knows.

And the same voice said, "Why, it's 'Erb."

Crashing back on the return journey, the limbers empty, 'Erb again bringing up the rear with the spares, one blinding flash, and –

We laid him in the gutter.

Did I not say that he came from the gutter? And to the gutter he returned in the fullness of time.

CHAPTER 10

The sixth drunk

"No. 10379 Private Michael O'Flannigan, you are charged, first, with being absent from roll-call on the 21st instant until 3.30 am on the 22nd, a period of five hours and thirty minutes; second, being drunk; third, assaulting an NCO in the execution of his duty."

The colonel leant back in his chair in the orderly-room and gazed through his eyeglass at the huge bullet-headed Irishman standing on the other side of the table.

The evidence was uninteresting, as such evidence usually is, the only humorous relief being afforded by the sergeant of the guard on the night of the 21st, who came in with an eye of cerulean hue which all the efforts of his painstaking wife with raw beefsteak had been unable to subdue. It appeared from his evidence that he and Private O'Flannigan had had a slight difference of opinion, and that the accused had struck him in the face with his fist.

"What have you got to say, Private O'Flannigan?"

"Shure, 'twas one of the boys from Waterford, sorr, I met in the town yonder, and we put away a bit of the shtuff. I would not be denying I was late, but I was not drunk at all. And as for the sergeant, sure 'twas messing me about he was and plaguing me, and I did but push him in the face. Would I be hitting him, and he a little one?"

The colonel glanced at the conduct sheet in his hand; then he looked up at O'Flannigan.

"Private O'Flannigan, this is your fifth drunk. In addition to that you have struck a non-commissioned officer in the execution of his duty, one of the most serious crimes a soldier can commit. I'm sick of you. You do nothing but give trouble. The next drunk you have I shall endeavour to get you discharged as incorrigible and worthless. As it is, I shall send you up for court-martial. Perhaps they will save me the trouble. March out."

"Prisoner and escort – right turn – quick march!" The sergeant-major piloted them through the door; the incident closed.

Now all that happened eighteen months ago. The rest is concerning the sixth drunk of Michael O'Flannigan and what he did; and it will also explain why at the present moment, in a certain depot mess in England, there lies in the centre of the dinner-table, every guest night, a strange jagged-looking piece of brown earthenware. It was brought home one day in December by an officer on leave, and it was handed over by him to the officer commanding the depot. And once a week officers belonging to the 13th and 14th and other battalions gaze upon the strange relic and drink a toast to the Sixth Drunk.

It seems that during November last the battalion was in the trenches round Ypres. Now, as all the world knows, at that time the trenches were scratchy, the weather was vile, and the Germans delivered infantry attacks without cessation. In fact, it was a most unpleasing and unsavoury period. In one of these scratchy trenches reposed the large bulk of Michael O'Flannigan. He did not like it at all – the permanent defensive which he and everyone else were forced into. It did not suit his character. Along with O'Flannigan there were a sergeant and three other men, and at certain periods of the day and night the huge Irishman would treat the world to an impromptu concert. He had a great deep bass voice, and when the mood was on him he would bellow out strange seditious songs – songs of the wilds of Ireland – and mingle with them taunts and jeers at the Germans opposite.

Now these bursts of song were erratic, but there was one period which never varied. The arrival of the rum issue was invariably heralded by the most seditious song in O'Flannigan's very seditious repertory.

One evening it came about that the Huns tactlessly decided to deliver an attack just about the same time as the rum was usually issued. For some time O'Flannigan had been thirstily eyeing the traverse in his trench round which it would come – when suddenly the burst of firing all along the line proclaimed an attack. Moreover, it was an attack in earnest. The Huns reached the trenches and got into them, and, though they were twice driven out, bit by bit the battalion retired. O'Flannigan's trench being at the end and more or less unconnected with the others, the Germans passed it by: though, as the sergeant in charge very rightly realised, it could only be a question of a very few minutes before it would be untenable.

"Get out," he ordered, "and join up with the regiment in the trenches behind."

"And phwat of the issue of rum?" demanded Michael O'Flannigan, whose rifle was too hot to hold.

"You may think yourself lucky, my bucko, if you ever get another," said the sergeant. "Get out."

O'Flannigan looked at him. "If you're after thinking that I would be leaving the rum to them swine you are mistaken, sergeant."

"Are you going, O'Flannigan?"

"Bedad, I'm not! Not if the King himself was asking me."

At that moment a Boche rounded the traverse. With a howl of joy O'Flannigan hit him with the butt of his rifle. From that moment he went mad. He hurled himself over the traverse and started. It was full of Germans – but this wild apparition finished them. Roaring like a bull and twisting his rifle round his head like a cane, the Irishman fell on them – and as they broke, he saw in the corner the well-beloved earthenware pot containing the rum. He seized the thing in his right hand and poured most of the liquid down his throat, while the rest of it ran over his face and clothes. And then Michael O'Flannigan ran amok. His great voice rose high above the roar of the rifles, as, with the empty rum jar in one hand and his clubbed rifle in the other he went down the trench.

What he must have looked like with the red liquid pouring down his face, his hands covered with it, his clothes dripping with it in that eerie half-light, Heaven knows. He was shouting an old song of the Fenian days, and it is possible they thought he was the devil. He was no bad substitute anyway. And then of a sudden his regiment ceased to shoot from the trenches behind and a voice cried, "O'Flannigan." It passed down the line, and, as one man, they came back howling, "O'Flannigan." They drove the Germans out like chaff and fell back into the lost trenches – all save one little party, who paused at the sight in front of them. There stood O'Flannigan astride the Colonel, who was mortally wounded. They heard rather than saw the blow that fetched home on the head of a Prussian officer – almost simultaneously with the crack of his revolver. They saw him go down with a crushed skull, while the big earthenware jar shivered to pieces. They saw O'Flannigan stagger a little and then look round – still with the top of the rum jar in his hand.

"You are back," he cried. "It is well, but the rum is gone."

And then the Colonel spoke. He was near death and wandering. "The regiment has never yet lost a trench. Has it, O'Flannigan, you scoundrel?" And he peered at him.

"It has not, sorr," answered the Irishman.

"I thought," muttered the dying officer, "there were Prussians in here a moment ago."

"They were, sorr, but they were not liking it, so they went."

Suddenly the Colonel raised himself on his elbow. "What's the matter with you, O'Flannigan? What's that red on your face? It's rum, you blackguard. You're drunk again." His voice was growing weaker. "Sixth time...discharged...incorrigible and worthless." And with that he died.

They looked at O'Flannigan, and he was sagging at the knees. "Bedad! 'tis not all rum, the red on me, Colonel, dear."

He slowly collapsed and lay still.

And that is the story of the strange table adornment of the depot mess, the depot of the regiment who have never yet lost a trench.

CHAPTER 11

The coward

James Dawlish's soul was sick within him. His tongue was cleaving to the roof of his mouth, parched and dry; his eyes gazed dully out of his white face at the pack of the man in front of him, who, like himself and fifty others, crouched huddled up in the ditch beside the road. Away in front stretched the *pavé* road, gleaming white in the dim light of dusk, the road that ran straight, as only French roads can, until, topping the rise three-quarters of a mile ahead, it merged into the darkness of the two lines of trees that guarded it. And twenty yards beyond that rise lay the German lines.

Then suddenly it came again. Out of the silent evening air the sudden salvo of six sharp hisses and six deafening cracks, the angry zipping of high explosive shrapnel through the trees over his head, the little eddies of dust in the road, the little thuds in the banks of the ditch where he crouched. Put baldly – in the language of the army – the Germans were searching the road with whizz-bangs, and had been doing so for twenty minutes. And the soul of James Dawlish was sick within him.

All around him men were muttering, laughing, cursing, each after his kind. In front an officer, very young, very new, was speaking to his sergeant-major. What he said is immaterial – which is perhaps as well, as he did nothing but repeat himself. The sergeant-major was a man of understanding, grown as used to shells as man may grow. For that matter so had the others – they were not a new regiment. James Dawlish was not new either. It was not his baptism of fire – he'd been shelled many times before; but for all that he was afraid – terribly, horribly afraid.

The psychology of fear is a strange thing. It is perhaps paradoxical, but I venture to think that without fear there can be no bravery – bravery, that is, in the true sense of the word. There are, I believe, some men who are without fear – literally and absolutely fearless. Such a condition of mind may be induced by sincere fatalism, but I rather think in the majority of cases it is due to a peculiar and fortunate twist of the brain. Inasmuch as one man will without thought dive forty feet into the sea and enjoy it, so will another, whose limbs would tremble at such a thought, boldly enter a cage of lions. Temperament, temperament only, at the bottom of it. And so it may well be that, were the wonderful, soul-stirring heroism of some VC to be weighed in the balance of mind and soul rather than in the balance of deed, he would be found less worthy to hold that coveted ribbon than a man whose sole contribution to fame was that he didn't run away.

Not so James Dawlish. With him fear seemed to be cumulative. Each time he came under fire, his terror of it increased. With most of us, who lay no claim to be without fear, sooner or later a merciful callousness settles down. Not that, if we think about it, our dislike of the *genus obus* is any less – far from it. But as time goes on, and a man does not get hit, though one day the dug-out he had just left was flattened by a crump, and another the man he was talking to was killed before his eyes; though he may have had a hundred narrow escapes, yet in time it becomes to a greater or less extent his natural element – a part and parcel of his life – a thing of routine as much as breakfast, more so, in some cases. But that man is no braver now than he was: more fearless, perhaps, but no braver. It is, then, with most of us, the factor of custom that pulls us through the mill, and preserves our reason.

But to James Dawlish that factor was denied. Fate had decreed that the brain of James Dawlish should be so fashioned that no immunity from death in the past should detract one iota from the hideous terror of death in the present. Every tour of duty in the trenches he died a thousand deaths. He saw himself left dying between the lines, stabbed in a sudden German rush, the recipient of the attentions of a Black Maria. He pictured to himself countless forms of death, each one more unpleasant than the last. Only the routine, the discipline of the army had held him up to date, that and the complete lack of opportunity to run away. It is easier said than done to run away from the front-line trenches, especially when things are quiet.

Which all boils down to the one essential fact that James Dawlish was a coward in the true sense of the word. Hundreds of men have lost their nerve temporarily, hundreds of men, huddled in a scratch in the ground, with their senses deadened and crushed by an inferno of bursting shells, have done things which the thoughtless dub cowardly. Men suddenly exposed to gas with no means of protection, men waking to find the trench full of liquid fire, these and countless other cases no man may judge unless he has stood beside them in similar circumstances and not been found wanting. But James Dawlish was not one of these. To him every moment of his life was a living death, a torture worse than hell. If one looks back to the cause of things, it was, I suppose, his misfortune and not his fault. He had been made so. Fear was a part of him, and pity rather than contempt is perhaps the fairest feeling to entertain for him. He could no more help his state of permanent terror, than a cat can help its dislike of water.

"Get up." The word came down the line, the shelling seemed to have stopped. The men in front of him were moving off up the road, but still he remained. A man tripped over him and cursed, but James Dawlish sat fumbling with his putties. No scheme was in his head; he had no intention of not going up to the front line; but clear out of the jumble of thoughts in his brain was his feverish desire to postpone if only for five minutes his nearer acquaintance with those great green flares that lobbed into the sky so near him. He could almost hear the faint hiss as they fell burning to the ground. God! how he hated it! Then they started shelling a crossroads a hundred yards behind him, and he cowered still closer in the ditch, almost whimpering – for it had suddenly struck him that he was alone. His platoon had gone on and left him: he had not even got the faint comfort of another man beside him. He was alone, utterly alone on a shell-swept road with an occasional spare bullet pinging down it, and the trees throwing fantastic shadows around him.

Then suddenly above his head he heard voices, and the soft thrumming of a motor.

"They'll stop hating in a moment and then we'll rush it," said a voice.

James Dawlish looked up, and in that moment the idea was born in his bemused brain. Safety – away from those cursed shells – away from those hissing green flares! What matter the right or wrong – what matter the penalties? Nothing entered into his calculations, saving only the thought of escape. And so with infinite caution he got out of the ditch and approached the driver of the ambulance as if he had been coming down the road.

"Give us a lift, mate, will you?" he asked casually.

"Right ho! hop in. They've stopped shelling." The ambulance was off – the driver unsuspicious. Many isolated men walk about behind the trenches at night, and anyway, it was none of his business.

Thus it came about that No. 1234 Private James Dawlish, of the second battalion of the Loamshires, when on active service, deserted His Majesty's Forces.

Now Thomas Atkins alone in a strange country, despite all rumours to the contrary, is a somewhat helpless individual. He will generally contrive to feed himself, and he has an infallible instinct for spotting those *estaminets* that contain the unpleasing liquid which passes as beer in Flanders. But when it comes to getting from one place to another, he gives up the unequal contest, and throws himself on the mercy of the nearest officer. And this was precisely what James Dawlish could not do. In the first place, he didn't know where he did want to go; he didn't much care so long as he kept out of the trenches; and in the second place, he was quite an old enough soldier to realise what he had done and, what was far more to the point, to realise the penalty. "Death or such less punishment as is in this Act mentioned."

Detection, he knew, would not come from the regiment. Too many men are reported missing for his absence to evoke any awkward questions. It was the people behind he had to fear, military police, assistant provost-marshals, and such-like abominations to the evil-doer. If only he could lie hid for a time, and finally borrow someone else's clothes and disappear – that was his half-formed play. Hazy and nebulous, true – but anything, anything on God's earth rather than go back.

It was while he was turning it over in his mind, with no clear idea of where he was going, that, rounding a bend in the road, he saw a few miles off the monastery that is set on a hill, and which forms one of the few noticeable landmarks in Flanders. The monastery where the cavalry had a skirmish in October last, and the monks in their brown cowls and cassocks buried the result. There were English troopers, and German Uhlans, and also there was a German Prince. And this monastery, set on the Mont des Cats, came back to James Dawlish as an old friend. Had he not billeted in the village at the foot of it with the unpronounceable name when he first came to the front?

No need now to ask his way – he would go back to the village – where there was a girl he knew of, and she would help him. And so with a comparatively light heart he started, and in the course of a few hours he found himself at the farm which had been his first resting-place in France.

Now, it is quite possible that, were it not for the extraordinary paucity of girls whom one may look at without smoked glasses in this delectable country, James Dawlish might have staved off the inevitable for quite a time. When he left the ambulance, he had carefully buried in a pond his rifle and equipment, and any-one meeting him strolling down the road would have taken him to be merely a man from a unit resting. To make things more sure, he had removed his cap badge, and the titles on his shoulder straps. There was nothing whatever to show what he belonged to; he was merely a disreputable atom of the big machine in much-damaged khaki. But, as I have said, there was a girl in the case, and moreover, she was a girl who had been very kind to James Dawlish earlier in the proceedings. She really had been quite fond of him, but when he went away and the place knew him no more, being a girl of common sense she transferred her attentions to his successor. As a matter of fact, there had been several successors, as regiments came and went, the intervals being filled with the semi-permanent sheet-anchor who stood for several hours each day at the crossroads by the church in the village with the unpronounceable name. And this sheet-anchor, who watched men come and watched men go, was a corporal in the Military Police.

It was during one of his innings with the fair maiden that James Dawlish tactlessly arrived on the scene; and when the corporal made his appearance in the evening, having successfully carried out his arduous duties regulating the traffic during the afternoon he found the object of his affections planted firmly in the arms of an extremely untidy and travel-stained private. It is perhaps unnecessary to state that, annoyed as the corporal was at this untoward intrusion on his preserves, his feelings were harmonious compared to those of Private Dawlish. To run full tilt into a Red Cap – as Tommy calls them – was the last thing he had intended doing; and a glance at the corporal's face told him that the corporal was out for blood.

"Who the 'ell are you, and what's your regiment?" he remarked tersely, looking at his badgeless cap.

And James Dawlish knew the game was up. He didn't even know what regiments were in the neighbourhood; if he had he might have lied and tried a bluff. So he said who he was, and named his regiment.

"The Loamshires?" said the corporal. "Second battalion? But they're in the trenches, for my brother's in that there battalion." The Military Policeman looked at him mercilessly. "What are you doing 'ere, my lad?"

And this time James Dawlish was silent: there was nothing to say. To an officer he'd have lied, uselessly, perhaps, but lied on principle: to a corporal he knew the futility. Two minutes later the door closed behind them, and they passed down the street.

Thus it came about that No. 1234 Private James Dawlish, of the second battalion of the Loamshires, was apprehended by the Military Police, and placed in the guard-room of the village with the unpronounceable name, to await the investigation of his case by the APM or assistant provost-marshal of the district.

And now the inevitable end must be written. There is not much to tell; the whole thing was plain. The APM investigated the case, and it stood revealed in its hideous bareness. There was not a single redeeming feature. It was no case of a man's nerve temporarily breaking under some fearful strain: where now, in the wisdom of those in high places, a man may work off his slur, by returning and trying again. It was just a simple case of cowardice and desertion in the presence of the enemy, and for it there was no excuse. That James Dawlish was made that way may have been his misfortune, but if that were taken as an excuse a good many men might find themselves sitting quietly in villages with unpronounceable names, while their pals lost their lives farther east.

So in due course James Dawlish stood before a court-martial. The evidence was heard, and then the accused was marched out, ignorant of his fate.

"The Court is closed to consider its finding." Thus spoke the President, a Major in the infantry. And when the door had closed, he turned to the junior member – a subaltern of gunners – and his face was grave. It is the law of courts-martial that the junior member gives his idea of the adequate sentence first, in order that he may not be influenced by what his seniors have said.

"What is your opinion?" asked the Major.

The subaltern drummed on the table with his fingers, and stared in front of him. Death, or such less penalty. The words seemed stamped on the wall. For a space he was silent; then he swallowed twice and spoke.

The Major glanced at the Captain, and the Captain, who was gazing fixedly out of the window, turned slowly round, and nodded. "I agree," he remarked incisively.

The Major looked at the papers in front of him, and mechanically produced his cigarette case. Then he wrote, and his hand shook a little.

And though the Major and the Captain and the subaltern had one and all looked on death many times unmoved, yet that night they were strangely silent.

To those who insist on the hundred and first chapter I can but quote the following bald announcement that appeared in a document of surprising dullness known as General Routine Orders. It had a number which I forget, and it was sandwiched between an interesting statement about exchanging French money into English, and a still more entrancing one on the subject of the Regimental Debts Act. Moreover, it was labelled Courts-Martial, and ran as follows:

No. 1234 Private James Dawlish, 2nd Battalion, The Loamshires, was tried by a Field General Courts-Martial on the following charge:

"When on active service deserting His Majesty's Service."

The sentence of the Court was "To suffer death by being shot."

The sentence was duly carried out at 4 a.m. on August 3rd.

And the only thing which gives a man to think is that about six hours after they laid that poor dishonoured clay in the ground, the manager of a large emporium at home was pleased to promote one of his shopwalkers from the glove department to a sphere of activity which concerned itself principally with stockings. I don't know why stockings were more highly paid than gloves in that emporium, but no matter.

The point of the thing is the shopwalker. His name is Dawlish – Augustus Dawlish. He used to look down on his brother James. Soldiering is not a genteel occupation compared to selling stockings. I suppose he'll do so still more if he ever learns the truth.

CHAPTER 12

Will you take over his horse, sir?

In the sky overhead the sun struggled through the drifting clouds, throwing a watery gleam on the sea of mud which called itself the picket line. Just for a moment it seemed as if it would triumph, and, as I looked up, the old bay horse with the batman standing at his head was bathed in sunshine. Behind him the troop horses steadily munching hay; the men in little scattered groups squatting round camp fires watching their dinners cook. Just the same as it was yesterday, just the same as it was the day before, but – "Will you take over his horse, sir?"

In the distance a black speck seemed to be hanging in the air. All round it little sharp flashes of fire and fleecy puffs of smoke showed that the Germans had also seen that speck and hoped it was within range. There was one complete set of six smoke balls, so close together that one could almost cover them with a soup plate. Another set had only five. Ah! there was the sixth, a little wide. There had been three perfect groups of six when he and I had been looking at the same thing a few mornings before. Listlessly I watched the black speck. Gradually it grew larger and larger until the big biplane passed overhead. And underneath the Union Jack – painted on the plane. Just the same, thank Heaven, just the same. The flag untouched, each unit which represents that flag carrying on the inexorable work. There is no cessation; there are others; it is war, but – "Will you take over his horse?"

The old bay horse! I wonder if you, too, remember that day at Tattersall's. Do you remember the hand running over your legs and stopping at that big splint on your off fore? Can you hear again that voice you've got to know so well? "Look at those hocks, man; look at that shoulder; that splint may just bring him down to my price." And do you remember the hunts? Do you remember that point-to-point when you both came such a crumpler at that big stake and biner? Perhaps you remember, old horse, perhaps you do; for who shall say just where an animal's knowledge begins and ends? There's no good your looking round like that. You haven't seen him this morning, have you? – and you know something's wrong, but you don't know what. How should you? You don't understand, and I do, Heaven knows – which is worse. In time perhaps the sugar will taste just as good out of my hand as far as you're concernèd. I hope it will, because – well, you heard the question, too – "Will you take over his horse?"

Yes, I must take you over until someone else can take you from me, if you come through this show alive. You don't know much about that someone, do you, old chap? Do you remember that day when you made such a fool of yourself because a side saddle had been put on you for the first time, and your master with a sack round his waist was sitting on your back all askew, as you thought. And then about a week after, when you were quite accustomed to it, someone else got upon you who was so light that you scarcely felt any weight at all. And when you lifted your heels a bit, just for fun, because you hardly knew there was anyone there at all, do you remember how he rubbed your muzzle, and talked to you until you became quiet? But there are so many things that you can't know, aren't there, old horse? You weren't in my room when he came round to it that night to tell me before anyone else of his wonderful luck. You couldn't know that the little light load you carried so often was the most precious thing in the whole world to the man who never missed coming round to your box after dinner on a hunting day, to make sure you were rugged up and bedded down for the night all right. That's where I get the pull of you, old man. You see, I was going to be his best man when he could afford to get married. He insisted on that when he told me first. But – things have happened since that night, and I'm going to take you over, because I want to give you back to her. I don't expect you'll carry her hunting again; women aren't made that way – at least not this one. Though he'd like it, I know.

But then, he won't be able to tell her. That's the rub. I know it was only yesterday afternoon you heard him say that it was a grand day for a hunt. I know it was only last night that you were saddled up suddenly with all the other troop horses and trotted for two hours along muddy roads in the darkness. Then he⁻ dismounted – didn't he? – and went on on foot with his men, while you and his other horse stopped behind. And you couldn't understand why a few hours later, when the other men mounted, no one got on your back, and you were led back here. Just a casual German sniper, sitting in a tree, taking pot shots into the darkness. Just a small round hole right in the centre of his forehead and the back of his head – but we won't think of that. That's what happened, old man. Nothing very glorious, nothing at all heroic. It's so ordinary, isn't it? It has already happened hundreds of times. It's going to happen hundreds more. Everything is going on just the same. It hasn't made any difference. The guns are in action just as they were yesterday, and there's that Maxim going again. But you've lost your master, old horse; and I've lost a friend: and the girl? – Not a bad bag, for half an ounce of lead!

They've left him up there, with a cross over his shallow grave, and his name scrawled on it with an indelible pencil. One can't get up there in the daylight – it's not safe. I'd like to have gone tonight to see if it was all right: but there's a job of work to be done elsewhere. So I'll have to lie to her. I'm writing her this afternoon. I can't let her open the paper one morning, and suddenly see his name standing out in letters of fire from all the others. Just a pawn in the game – another officer killed – a bare, hard fact, brutal, uncompromising. No more letters to look forward to: no more socks and smokes to send out. True, the socks never fitted, but she didn't know. No: I can't let her find it out that way. I must write: though what on earth can I say to her? I never could write a letter like that. If you're going to have your head smashed with a sledgehammer, one can't do much to deaden the blow. But I'll tell her I've seen his grave, and that it's all right. Just a pawn in the game. Only he was her king.

"Will you take over his horse, sir? Your chestnut is very lame in front."

Teddy, old man, I've hunted with you: I've shot with you: I've played cricket with you: I've made love with you. You were one of Nature's sportsmen: one of the salt of the earth. May the earth lie lightly on you, old pal. There's a motor-cyclist coming with orders now: the same fellow with spectacles who has been to us for the last fortnight. There's a Taube overhead, and the infantry are loosing off at it. It's out of range, just the same as usual. Everything is just the same, Teddy, except that someone's heart has got to be broken, and that I – well, I've taken over your horse.

CHAPTER 13

Morphia

The man stirred uneasily, and a faint moan came from his lips. A numbness seemed to envelop his body from the waist downwards, and in the intervals of a stabbing pain in his head, he seemed to hear people whispering near by. A figure passed close to him, the figure of a girl with fair hair, in a grey dress – the figure of a girl like Molly. A red-hot iron stabbed his brain; his teeth clenched on his lips; he fought with all his will, but once again he moaned; he couldn't help it – it was involuntary. The girl stopped and came towards him, for he heard her voice. But what was she saying? Why did she speak so indistinctly? Why – ah, but her hand on his forehead was cool. It seemed to quiet those raging devils in his head; it helped him, as Molly always helped him. It seemed to – why, surely, it must be Molly herself, with her dear, soft touch, and her lips ready to kiss, and the sweet smell of her hair mounting to his brain like wine. Something pricked his arm: something that felt like the needle of a syringe; something that… But anyway, what the deuce was she doing? Then suddenly he recalled that pin at the back of her dress, where he'd pricked his wrist so badly the first time he'd kissed her.

He laughed gently at the remembrance; and the hand on his forehead trembled. For laughter to be a pleasant thing to hear it is essential that the person who laughs should be in full possession of – well, it is better, at any rate, that his head should not have been hit by a bomb, especially if it was his lower jaw that bore the brunt.

"What are you trembling for, Molly?" The voice was tender. "The pain has quite gone – I must have had a touch of the sun."

But for a question to be answered it must be audible; and the girl whose hand was on his forehead heard no words. Merely was there a great and wonderful pity in her eyes, for the remnant – the torn-up remnant – who had fought and suffered for her. And the remnant, well, he was way back in the Land of Has-been. Did I not say that the pin was at the back of Molly's waist?

The woods were just at their best, with the glorious yellow and brown of early autumn, touched with the gold of the setting sun. In a clearing a boy was sitting on a fallen tree trunk, puffing furiously at a cigarette. Twice had the smoke gone the wrong way, and once had it got into his eyes; but when one is aged sixteen such trifles are merely there to be overcome. The annoying thing was that he was still engaged in absorbing the overflowing moisture from his eyes, with a handkerchief of doubtful cleanliness, when a girl came into the glade and started to laugh.

"There's no good pretending, Billy. The smoke has got into your eyes, and your handkerchief is dirty, and you aren't impressing me in the slightest."

"Hallo, Molly! I wasn't expecting you so soon." The smoker looked a little sheepish.

"Indeed! Then if I'm not wanted, I'll go away again."

"No, no, Molly – don't do that." The boy rose eagerly, and went towards her. Then he stopped awkwardly, and putting his hands in his pockets, fidgeted with his feet.

"Well – why not?" The girl smiled provokingly. "And what are you hopping about for? Are you going to try to learn to dance, as I suggested?"

"I will if you will teach me, Molly – dear." He took a step forward eagerly – and then paused again, aghast at the audacity of that "dear." Something in the cool, fresh young girl standing so easily in front of him, smiling with faint derision, seemed to knock on the head all that carefully thought out plan which had matured in his mind during the silent watches of the previous night. It had all seemed so easy then. Johnson major's philosophy on life in general and girls in particular was one thing in the abstract, and quite another when viewed in the concrete, with a real, live specimen to practise on. And yet Johnson major was a man of much experience – and a prefect of some standing at school.

"My dear fellows," he had said on one occasion when holding the floor in his study, "I don't want to brag, and *we* do not speak about these things." The accent on the *we* had been wonderful. It implied membership of that great body of youthful daredevils to whom the wiles of women present no terrors. "But women, my dear fellows, why – good lord, there's nothing in it when one knows the way to manage them. They adore being kissed – provided it's done the right way. And if you don't know the right way instinctively, it comes with practice, old boy, it comes with practice." Billy had listened in awe, though preserving sufficient presence of mind to agree with the speaker in words of suitable nonchalance.

Of course, Johnson major must have been right; but, devil take it, there seemed remarkably little instinct available at the present moment; and up to date in Billy's career, practice in the proper procedure had been conspicuous by its absence.

"I think you're rather dull today." The girl was speaking again, and there was more than a hint of laughter in her voice. "What's the matter with you? Has the cigarette made you feel sick?"

"Certainly not. I – er – oh, Molly, I – "

124

The desperate words trembled on his lips – trembled and died away under the laughter in her eyes.

"Yes?" she murmured inquiringly. "What is it, Billy?"

Oh, woman, woman! Just sixteen, but at two you have learned the beginnings of the book of Eve.

"I – er – I – oh, dash it, let's go for a walk!" With a gasp of relief he swung on his heel; the fatal plunge had been put off for a little; he hadn't made a fool of himself – yet, at any rate. "Do you mind if I smoke?"

"Not if you don't." The girl was walking demurely beside him, down the narrow lane carpeted with its first layers of auburn brown. "Are you sure it's wise? Two so close together might not be good for you."

Two close together – not good for him! Absurd; it was nothing to what he was accustomed to, and yet – why, his head was throbbing, throbbing as he looked at the girl beside him? What was that distant noise like the slow beating of a mighty drum, that seemed to quiver and vibrate in the air till it filled his brain with a great rush of sound, and then sobbed away into silence? What was the matter with his right hand that it burned and twitched so ceaselessly? Surely he hadn't burnt himself with the cigarette! He looked down to see, but somehow things were indistinct. It almost seemed as if he hadn't got a hand; the woods were hazy – Molly seemed far away. In her place was a man, a man with a stubby growth on his chin, a man who bent over him and muttered something.

"Gawd, Ginger, the poor devil ain't dead neither! Lift him up carefully. There's his right arm over there, and his back – Oh, my gawd! Poor devil!"

Thus had the battalion stretcher-bearers found him the day before...

The man became irritable.

"Go away at once! Can't you see I'm with a lady. Molly, dear, where are you? What is this dirty-looking fellow doing here at all?"

But Molly for the moment seemed aloof. He saw her there, standing in the path in front of him – so close and yet somehow so curiously far away.

"Molly, do you hear that noise – that strange beating in the air? I think I'm going to be ill. Perhaps two close together are too much."

But no – apparently not. Suddenly everything was clear again, and there was Molly with the autumn wind blowing the soft tendrils of hair back from the nape of her neck; Molly, with the skirt that betokens the halfway period between flapperhood and coming out; Molly, with her lithe young figure half turned from him as she watched the sun sinking over the distant hills.

"They adore being kissed." The words of the wonderful Johnson major were ringing in his brain as he watched her, and suddenly something surged up within him. What matter rules and theories? What matter practice? There is only one way to kiss a girl, and rules and theories avail not one jot. With a quick step he had her in his arms, and, with his pulses hammering with the wonder of it, he watched her face come round to his. He kissed her cheek, her eyes, her mouth – shyly at first, and then with gathering confidence as a boy should kiss a girl.

The sweetness of it, the newness of it, the eternal joy of a woman in a man's arms for the first time! Surely it had never been quite like that with anyone else before. Of course, other people kissed, but – this was different. Suddenly the girl disengaged her arms and wound them gently round his neck. She pulled his head towards her, and kissed him again and again, while he felt her heart beating against his coat.

"Billy, my dear!"

Almost he missed the whispered words coming faintly from somewhere in the neighbourhood of his tie.

"Molly – Molly, darling – I love you!"

The boy's voice was shaky, his grip almost crushed her.

"Do you, Billy? I'm so glad! I want you to love me, because – because – "

She looked at him shyly.

"Say it, sweetheart, say it." He held her at arm's-length – no longer bashful, no longer wondering whether he dared; but insistent, imperious, a young god for the moment. "Because what?"

"Because I love you too, you darling!"

Once again she was in his arms, once again did time cease, while the lengthening shadows stole softly towards them; and a squirrel, emboldened by their stillness, watched for a while with indulgent eyes.

At last the girl turned gently away, and the boy's arms fell to his side.

"Molly, you've got a pin in your waistband. Look, you've pricked my wrist."

"Billy, my dear, let me do it up. Why didn't you tell me, you poor old boy?"

"I didn't notice it, I didn't even feel it, you darling."

The boy laughed gladly as she bound his handkerchief round the wounded arm; and, bending forward, kissed her neck, just where the hair left it, just where – but what had happened? Where was she? She had gone, the trees had gone, the sun had set, and it was dark, terribly dark.

Once again that mighty drum beat close by, and voices came dimly through a haze to the man's brain. Someone was touching him, a finger was probing gently over his head, a sentence came to him as if from a vast distance.

"Good God! Poor devil! If we have to go we must leave him. Any movement would kill him at once."

"I won't have you touching the bandage that Molly put on!" said the man angrily. "My wrist will be quite all right; it's absurd to make a fuss about a pin-prick."

And perhaps because there are sounds to which no man can listen unmoved, the quiet-faced doctor drew out his hypodermic syringe. The girl with the grey dress, her steps lagging a little with utter physical weariness, paused at the foot of the bed, and waited with an encouraging smile.

"Molly," he cried eagerly, "come and talk to me! I've been dreaming about you."

But she merely continued to smile at him, though in her eyes there was the sadness of a divine pity. Then once again something pricked his arm. A great silence seemed to come down on him like a pall, a silence that was tangible, in which strange faces passed before him in a jumbled procession. They seemed to swing past like fishes drifting across the glass window of an aquarium – ghostly, mysterious, and yet very real. A man in a dirty grey uniform, with a bloodstained bandage round his forehead, who leered at him; Chilcote, his company commander, who seemed to be shouting and cheering and waving his arm; a sergeant of his platoon, with a grim smile on his face, who held a rifle with a fixed bayonet that dripped.

"All right, Chilcote," he shouted, "we'll have the swine out in a minute!"

But Chilcote had gone, and through the silence came a muffled roar.

"The drum again!" he muttered irritably. "What the devil is the good of trying to surprise the Huns if we have the band with us! You don't want a band when you're attacking a village! A band is for marching to, and dancing, not for fighting." Of course, if it was going to continue playing, they might just as well have a dance, and be done with it. He laughed a little. "You've had too much champagne for supper, my boy," he soliloquised. "What do you mean by 'might as well have a dance'? Can't you see that awe-inspiring gentleman in the red coat is on the point of striking up now?" He looked across the room, a room that seemed a trifle hazy, and thought hard. Surely he hadn't had too much to drink, and yet the people were so vague and unreal? And why the deuce did a ballroom band have a big drum? He gave it up after a moment, and silently watched the scene.

He remembered now quite clearly, and with an amused laugh at his momentary forgetfulness, he looked at his programme. The third supper extra was just beginning, and two dances after that he had four in succession with Molly – the fateful hour when he had determined to try his luck.

At present she was having supper with a nasty-looking man, with long hair and an eyeglass, who was reputed to be a rising politician, in the running for an under-secretaryship, and was also reputed to be in love with Molly. He looked savagely round the room, and, having failed to discover them, he strolled to the bar to get a drink.

"Hallo, Billy; not dancing? She loves me; she loves me not! Cheer up, dearie!"

An inane-looking ass raised his whisky-and-soda to his lips with a fatuous cackle.

"I wonder they don't have a home for people like you, Jackson," remarked Billy curtly. "Whisky-and-soda, please."

He gave his order to the waiter and lit a cigarette. He hardly knew what the irrepressible Jackson was saying, but allowed him to babble on in peace while his thoughts centred on Molly. How absolutely sweet she was looking in that shimmering, gauzy stuff that just went with her hair, and showed off her figure to perfection! If only she said "yes," he'd arrange the party going back in the cars so that he got her alone in the two-seater. If only – good lord, would the dance never come?

He looked up, and saw her passing into the ballroom with her supper partner; and, as he did so, she looked half round and caught his eye. Just a second, no more; but on her lips had trembled the faintest suspicion of a smile – a smile that caused his heart to beat madly with hope, a smile that said things. He sat back in his chair and the hand that held his glass trembled a little.

"I don't believe you've been listening to me, Billy." The egregious Jackson emitted a plaintive wail. "I don't believe you've heard a word I said!"

"Perfectly correct in both statements, dear boy!" Billy rose abruptly to his feet and smacked him on the back. "One must give up something in Lent, you know."

"But it isn't Lent." Jackson looked aggrieved. "And you've made me spill my drink."

But he spoke to the empty air and a melancholy waiter, for Billy was back in the ballroom, waiting…

"You smiled at me, lady, a while ago," he said softly in her ear, as they swung gently through the crowded room. "I thought it was a smile that said things. Was thy servant very presumptuous in thus reading his queen's glance? Confound you, sir; that's my back!"

He glared furiously at a bull-necked thruster in a pink coat.

"Hush, Billy!" laughed the girl, as they lost him in the crowd. "That's our master!"

"I don't care a hang who he is, but he's rammed one of my brace-buttons into my spine! He's the sort of man who knocks you down and tramples on your face, after supper!"

For a few moments they continued in silence, perhaps the two best dancers in the room, and gradually she seemed to come closer to him, to give herself entirely up to him, until, as in a dream, they moved like one being and the music softly died away. For a moment the man stood still, pressing the girl close to him, and then, with a slight sigh that was almost one of pain, he let her go.

"Are you glad I taught you to dance?" she asked laughingly; while the room shouted for an encore.

"Glad," he whispered, "glad! Ah, my dear, my dear, to dance with you is the nearest approach to heaven that we poor mortals may have! For all that" – he steered her swiftly through the expectant couples towards a door covered with a curtain – "I want an answer to a question I asked you just before my spine was broken!" He held up the curtain for her to pass through, and piloted her to an easy chair hidden behind some screens in a discreetly lighted room. "Did your smile say things, my dear? Did you tell me something as you went into the ballroom with that long-haired lawyer?"

"My dear boy, I wasn't smiling at you! I was smiling at that nice Mr Jackson man."

"Molly, you're a liar! You know you hate that ass; as you told me yourself yesterday!"

"All the more reason to smile at him. Billy, give me a cigarette." She leaned towards him slightly as he offered her his case, and their eyes met. Her breath came a little quicker as she read the message blazing out of his, and then she looked away again. "And a match, please," she continued quietly.

"Confound the match and the cigarette, too!" His voice was shaking. "Molly, Molly, I know I'm mad! I know it's just the height of idiocy from a so-called worldly point of view, but I can't help it. I've tried and struggled; I've been away for two years and haven't seen you. But oh, my dear, the kisses you gave me when you were a flapper, before you came out, before your mother got this bee in her bonnet about some big marriage for you – those kisses are still burning my lips! I can feel them now, princess, and the remembrance of 'em drives me mad! I know I'm asking you to chuck your mother's ambitions; I know I've got nothing to offer you, except the old name, which don't count for much these days. But, oh, my beloved, I just worship the very ground you walk on! Is there just a chance for me? I'd simply slave for you, if you'd let me!"

Through the closed door came stealing the soft music of a waltz, while from another corner came the sound of a whispered *tête-à-tête*. Very still was the girl as she sat in the big armchair with the man pleading passionately at her side. Once she caught her breath quickly when he recalled the time gone by – the time before her mother's political ambitions had ruthlessly waged war on her, and done their best to drive nature out of her outlook on life; and, when he had finished speaking, she gave a little tired smile.

"Billy boy," she whispered, "is that how you've felt about it all this while?"

He made no answer, but, stretching out his hands, he took hold of her two wrists.

"You've really remembered those kisses when we were kids?" she went on softly.

"Remembered them? Dear heavens, my darling, I wouldn't lose that remembrance for untold wealth! It's been with me in Alaska; it's been with me in Hong-Kong. I've woken up at nights with the feel of your lips on mine, and all the glory of you, and the sweetness; and it's helped me on when everything was black, and made things bright when the world was rotten!" With a bitter sigh he took his hands away and sat back in his chair. "And I've failed! Jove! the wild schemes and the plans, the golden visions and the El Dorados – all failed. Just a little money, just enough to have a burst in England, just enough to be able to see you. And then it slipped out. My dear, I never meant to before I came to the Towers. I knew you were there, but I never meant to ask you. Wash it out, my princess; wash it out! I haven't said a word. You've been teaching me a new step; let's go back and dance. I've been mad this evening, and, unless we go back and dance, I can't guarantee remaining sane!"

But the girl made no move. With parted lips she swayed towards him, while he watched her, with the veins standing out on his forehead. "Billy – I don't care; I'm mad, too!" The scent she used was mounting to his brain – the nearness of her was driving him mad.

"Molly, get back to that ballroom; get back quick, or – " He spoke through his clenched teeth.

"Or what, Billy boy?" She smiled deliciously.

And then he kissed her; a kiss that seemed to draw her soul to her lips; a kiss that lifted him until he travelled through endless spaces in a great aching void where time and distance ceased, and nothing happened save a wonderful ecstasy, and ever and anon the mighty booming of a giant drum.

He seemed to be treading on air, and though the ballroom had vanished, and the discreet apartment with shaded lights had faded away, yet he was very conscious of the nearness of his girl. But just now, he could not see her – she eluded him, leaving an ever-present feeling that she would be waiting for him round the next of those intangible masses he seemed to be drifting through.

"You don't mind waiting, my princess?" he murmured ceaselessly. "After this war it will all come right. Just now I've got to go – I must go out there; but afterwards, it will all come right – and we'll live in a house in the country and grow cabbages and pigs. You'll wait, you say? Ah! my dear, my dear; it's sweet of you; but perhaps you ought to have married the lawyer man. You might have been Mrs Prime Minister one of these days."

For a while the tired brain refused to act; the man felt himself falling into unplumbed depths – depths which echoed with monstrous reverberations.

"Molly, where are you, dear? It's cold, and my head is throbbing to beat the band. If only that cursed drum would stop! Do you hear it echoing through the air? And the noise hurts – hurts like hell, Molly. Ah! Heaven, but it's cold; and I can't see you, beloved; I don't know where you are."

Once again he became conscious of figures moving around him. They seemed to be carrying motionless men past his feet – men on stretchers covered with blankets. With staring eyes he watched the proceeding, trying to understand what was happening. In front of him was a window in which the glass had been smashed, leaving great jagged pieces sticking out from the sides of the frame. He wondered vaguely why it had been left in such a dangerous condition; when he and Molly had their house such a thing would never be allowed to happen – if it did it would be mended at once. He asked one of the passing figures what had caused the damage, and when he got no answer he angrily repeated the question.

He fretted irritably because no one seemed to take any notice of him, and suddenly his head began throbbing worse than ever. But the hazy indistinctness was gone; the man was acutely conscious of everything around him. Memory had come back, and he knew where he was and why he was there. He remembered the fierce artillery bombardment; he recalled getting over the parapet, out on to the brown shell-pocked earth, sodden and heavy with the drenching rain; he recalled the steady shamble over the ground with boots so coated with wet mud that they seemed to drag him back. Then clear in his mind came the picture of Chilcote cheering, shouting, lifting them on to the ruins of what once had been a village; he saw Chilcote falter, stop, and, with a curious spinning movement, crash forward on to his face; he saw the Germans – he saw fierce-faced men like animals at bay, snarling, fighting; he heard once again that trembling cry of "*Kamarade*"; and then – a blank. The amazing thing was that it was all jumbled up with Molly. He seemed to have been with her lately – and yet she couldn't have been out there with him. He puzzled a bit, and then gave it up: it hurt his head so terribly to think. He just lay still, gazing fixedly at the jagged, torn pane of glass…

"They are all out, doctor, except this one."

A woman was speaking close beside him, and his eyes slowly travelled in the direction of the voice. It was another woman – a woman he hadn't seen before – swaying slightly as if she would drop.

"Good heavens! it's Billy Saunders!"

A man in khaki was bending over him – a man whom he recognised as a civilian doctor he'd known at home – a man, moreover, who knew Molly.

"Do you know me, old chap?"

"Of course," answered the man. "What's all the trouble?"

The doctor bit his lip, and the man noticed his hand clench hard. Then there started a low-voiced conversation to which he listened attentively – his hearing seemed abnormally acute.

"Has he spoken since he's been in, sister?"

"No – only those dreadful moans. The whole of his face – absolutely hopeless – spinal cord."

The man lying motionless caught the disjointed words. What did they mean? They were mad – insane. Dying? He – Billy Saunders! What about Molly – his Molly? What about… Gentle fingers once again touched his head, and, looking up, he saw the doctor's eyes fixed on his.

"They're shelling the hospital, dear old man; we've got to get – Great Scott, look out!"

Like the moan of a giant insect, the shrill whine came through the air, rising to an overwhelming scream. There was a deafening crash – a great hole was torn in the wall just by the window with the jagged pane, and the room filled with stifling black fumes. A sudden agonising stab, and the man, looking up, saw Molly in front of him. She was standing in the acrid smoke – beckoning.

"I'm coming, dear, I'm coming!" he cried; "it's good of you to have waited, girl of mine – so good."

"Are you hurt, sister?" The doctor, who had been crouching by the bed, stood up.

"Not touched, thank you." She was white and shaking. "Did you hear the bits whizzing through the room?"

"I did," remarked the doctor grimly, holding out an arm from which the blood already dripped. "And I felt one of them too. But there's no time to lose – I don't know what to do about him, poor old chap."

He turned once again to the bed, and even as he turned he knew the decision had been made for him: and he thanked the Maker. Billy Saunders had also felt a bit – a jagged bit – through the heart.

CHAPTER 14

The booby-trap

The trouble is that in War retribution so rarely comes on the man who deserves it. The thing is such an impersonal affair: shells, trench mortars, and rifle bullets slay or miss impartially, and there are so many pawns the less to carry on the good work. Even the bayonet cannot be said to settle any long-standing feud: the gentleman who dies and the gentleman who kills him are really complete strangers. Very annoyed with one another undoubtedly; but there is no question of the grievance being an old one.

And so, when some act of poetic justice is done, it is apt to impress itself forcibly on the memory. They are very rare, those acts: opportunities are few and far between. But sometimes they do, and… However, this was the way of one such occasion.

The name of the village is immaterial. It lies in the country evacuated by the Hun during February and March of 1917, and it is not yet marked on the small-scale maps. For the beginning of the affair one must go back to a certain night in March, twenty days after the Germans had gone. They had left it, as they left most of the villages in that district, destroyed but not gutted. The trees were cut, the little bits of garden were ruined, and the inhabitants bore in their eyes the hopeless despair, the frozen apathy, of those who have been down into the pit. Old and decrepit – for of their children none save babies remained – they sat about round the doors of their ruined houses, hardly speaking, just watching and wondering. To them had come the desolation of war, in full measure pressed down and running over, and the poor old tired brains could scarcely grasp it. The fruit of years, a whole life's work gone – finished; and no one to build it up again. Just them and a few little children – and desolation. Old men would mutter *soixante-dix*: old wives would shake their heads, wiping their eyes furtively with their aprons: the babies would stare solemnly and fearfully at the khaki soldiers who had replaced the field grey. For the spirit of Death does not leave those who live with it in a moment...

Now, in this particular village, on the day in question, were the headquarters of two battalions of infantry. The battalions in question were the Royal Loamshires and the South Devons, and from time immemorial the Loamshires and the South Devons had been friends. In the days before the war this friendship manifested itself in many ways, which it were, perhaps, indiscreet to mention. There was the occasion, for instance, when a battalion of the Loamshires, homeward bound after many years abroad, stopped for the night at a certain port of call where a battalion of the South Devons had its temporary residence. And there was a dinner to mark the happy occasion.

It has been handed on, the account of that dinner, in the archives of both these famous regiments. The unfortunate mishap which caused a distinguished general, specially invited for the occasion, to be greeted with an over-ripe melon in the chest just as he entered the ante-room; the sudden disappearance of the visiting colonel as he was making his fourth speech owing to his being torpedoed by an enterprising officer under the table; the celebrated feat of a subaltern who rode his bicycle five times round the billiard-table while other enthusiasts tried to poke him off with cues – all these and many like bonds to friendship occurred that night and on other gala occasions.

So it is not surprising that such a regimental tradition, founded and cemented in times of peace, should endure in the stress of war, and be passed on to the Service battalions for guidance and future action. Owing to circumstances beyond our control, ripe melons and billiard-tables are no longer available; but much may be done in the local *estaminet* where the omelette is good and the red wine better – where Madame's coffee is superb and the Benedictine comforting. Moreover, the two battalions with which we are concerned were quite alive to that fact.

Their friendship, however, did not prevent the really serious matters of life being taken with due solemnity. When a move was contemplated, the rival billeting officers became for the time sworn enemies. They vied with one another in lying and contumely to obtain the best accommodation for their own people, and the state of the score at the time showed that the South Devons were two up. That last point had rankled dreadfully with Finlayson, of the Loamshires: he swore that it was entirely due to the Town Major of the place where it occurred being soft in the head: he swore – many things, but the fact remained he was two down. And so when he discovered the battalion's destination, and further elicited from the Staff captain that they might be there anything from one hour to four days – the Staff captain disliked being a false prophet – he again swore. He swore a mighty vow that if Tremayne, of the South Devons, again did him down in the race for billets – which, in this case, were likely to prove even more sketchy than usual – thereby making the score three up, he personally would murder him with his own hand. Then he went and dined with him and discussed "Blighty."

By what vile deceit he succeeded is neither here nor there. All that is known officially is that Tremayne approached the village some half an hour after Finlayson had arrived, and that he looked thoughtful. Occasionally his lips moved – it is to be assumed in silent prayer; occasionally he raised a protesting hand to heaven and jibbered feverishly. He was met on the outskirts by Finlayson, smoking a fat cigar and smiling offensively.

"Good ride, dear old boy? I'm afraid you'll find the billeting accommodation a bit limited."

Tremayne dismounted in silence. "James," he remarked slowly, "I wouldn't have believed it of you. After all these years, to treat me thus – me, your almost brother! Why, you damned old scoundrel!…"

Finlayson held up a protesting hand. "This language grieves me to the quick, Peter. And the score is now one."

They stopped in front of the only decent-looking house in the village, and Tremayne inspected it with a professional eye. "Two windows, no door, a leaking roof. Great Scott! Old boy, I suppose that is where we've got to go?"

But Finlayson was not to be drawn. "Not so, Peter," he answered; "that is where we *have* gone. Yours is far worse – just down the road here. You haven't got a window at all!"

"Do you really mean this is the next best?" Tremayne demanded, when he had fully explored the second selection down the road. "The bally place is a series of holes indifferently held together by plaster!"

"I've had a good look round, and you won't find anything better." Finlayson gently fell through the wall he was leaning against and swore, while Tremayne pondered pessimistically. Under the rules of the game they did one another down only in so far as to who got the first pick. After that the second would be chosen by the conqueror with punctilious care and held against all corners till his rival should arrive.

"I would like," murmured Tremayne, when the other emerged from the debris, "to catch the Hun that did this."

"We have got a kitchen of sorts," spluttered Finlayson, at length, "so you'd better all lunch with us."

And this occurred on the twentieth day after the Germans had gone. On the twenty-first the two battalions were still there. The

Staff captain had arrived – principally to find how the score stood – and had left again. The Sapper commanding the Field company had arrived ostensibly to find if he could help anybody – in reality, to cadge lunch. The men, strolling aimlessly about, were fraternising with the inhabitants; and over the village there brooded an air of peace. The guns were more or less silent, and not too near; the aeroplanes seemed to be taking a day off, when – of a sudden, it occurred.

A rumbling, shaking roar; a great sheet of flame, and a belching cloud of dust; a rending sort of crash, as timbers and walls were torn asunder; the sound as of a mighty hailstorm, as bricks and rubble came raining down into the street; and it was over. The headquarters of the Royal Loamshires had ceased to exist. The house had disappeared, and in its place there hung a thick cloud of acrid smoke.

Mortimer, the CO of the South Devons, who was just preparing for his afternoon siesta, dashed into the road, colliding with his adjutant and Tremayne.

"What the devil was that?" he cried, only to stop abruptly and stare at the slowly-drifting pall of smoke. "My God! What's happened?"

From all directions men had come into the street, out of houses and barns, to see what had occurred. There had been no whine of a big shell; in the sky above there was no sign of an aeroplane; and yet a house had suddenly disappeared, and bits of it were still coming down, hitting the ground with a vicious thud.

Tremayne was the first to recover himself and walk up the village street towards the scene of the disaster. The roof had been completely blown off, and of the outside walls nothing except a few jagged splinters remained. A great mass of broken bricks and rubble blocked the near side of the road, filling the bottom story of the house; and, even as he approached, a big lump of brickwork broke off from the top of a still standing corner and narrowly escaped braining him as it fell.

But this was no time to worry about trifles of that sort. Only half an hour previously had he been lunching there with Finlayson and the CO and adjutant of the Loamshires. The doctor had been there, and the interpreter, and two or three other pals. Only, as I say, that had been half an hour ago.

Tremayne clambered up over the heap of debris, and almost at once he saw what caused him to curse savagely – an arm stuck out from the top. He hurled away the bricks which covered the rest from view and recognised what he found by the badges on the uniform. It was the doctor. Then he cursed again and turned to the Colonel, who was standing in the road behind.

"We'll want a fatigue-party, sir," he said. "I've found the doctor, and I'm afraid they're all in here, buried."

The Colonel nodded, and gave a brief order to his adjutant. Then he turned to the Field Company officer beside him. "What the devil do you think did it?" he asked.

"No shell, no aeroplane; it can only have been one thing." The Sapper thoughtfully studied the wreckage. "No shell except the very biggest could have made such a mess, and everyone would have heard it coming. No aeroplane bomb could have done it either. The Huns, before they left, laid a delay-action mine under the house, and it's just gone off."

"But it's twenty-one days, my dear chap!" objected Tremayne, who had joined them and heard the last remark.

"With a little ingenuity you could arrange a delay-action mine for twenty-one weeks," returned the engineer. "A question of acid eating through wire – connection being made when the wire severs. That's only one of many ways, and the time would depend entirely on the strength of the acid and the thickness of the wire. They knew this village would be occupied; they knew that that house, being the best available, would be occupied by an officers' mess. And the swine have drawn a winner."

In silence they watched the salvage operations, which were being directed by the adjutant.

"Just to think of the rotten luck of the thing!" burst out Tremayne suddenly. "Poor old Jimmy Finlayson – so damned pleased at having got the bulge on me and got this house. And now this happens! By Jove! There is the old boy now!"

He went to help two of the men who were carrying into the road all that was left of Finlayson, billeting officer of the Royal Loamshires.

"Carefully, boys," said Tremayne. "Lay him down there beside the doctor." For a while he looked at his dead friend in silence, and then he bent down and covered up his face with a handkerchief. "If," he remarked quietly to the Sapper officer, "I was ever privileged to meet the man who ordered that mine to be laid, he would die – nastily. Unfortunately, those things don't happen except in stories."

"No," replied the Sapper. "I'm afraid they don't."

Now we come to what happened on the twenty-second day in that little village in the evacuated area. The ball was started rolling during a stroll which Tremayne and the adjutant took before lunch. To all outward appearance the village was normal again; tragedies, however sudden, lose much of their sting when they happen in the Land of the Great Tragedy. At intervals heaps of brickwork from the tottering walls slithered down on the *pavé* below, raising a little cloud of dust; at intervals some old peasant would look with quavering eyes at the ruin by the corner and mumble foolishly to his wife. To them it was all part and parcel of the whole scheme of things – just one more of the upheavals in which they had lived for the past two years. Stray limbers still clattered down the street; limbers whose drivers never turned their heads to look at the heap of rubbish as they passed it. Similar heaps were too common to excite even the most casual remark. Lorries jolted on their way unheeding; dispatch-riders, in their khaki overalls, rushed past on bumping motor-bicycles; the normal life of France six miles behind the line, which must not be dislocated even for a second, carried on as usual.

Tremayne and the adjutant came to the end of the village, and paused for a moment in front of the last house. In silence they glanced at the fruit-trees, each with the usual ring cut round it; with a cynical smile they noticed the little bit of garden systematically and thoroughly destroyed.

"By George," remarked the adjutant thoughtfully, "those swine are thorough! They make a business of it, at any rate. What would you give, Peter, to do this to them in Germany?"

"We will, some day," Tremayne was always an optimist. "Always provided the peace swine at home are deleted from the book of the words. But, to come to more intimate details, Ginger, this house looks to me a great deal better than the one we're in at present. It has, at any rate, a window – and a door. Let us explore."

He pushed open the gate and, followed by the adjutant, walked into the front room. It was bare and mouldering, but the walls were intact, and so was the window.

"Not so bad!" exclaimed the adjutant. "With a fire and a tot of rum. By Jove, old boy, look at this! What about that for a mess-room?"

Tremayne peered over his shoulder as he stood in the open doorway of the room behind. It was a typical French kitchen, with old wood rafters and big stove all complete. In the centre was a table, with four or five chairs, and the remains of a meal, covered thickly with dust, were scattered about. Some German equipment was thrown in a corner, along with a few books, and close by the door there stood several bottles of beer. The room gave the appearance of having been suddenly left. All the chairs were pushed back from the table just as they would have been had their occupants suddenly risen and not returned. The beer in the glasses was half drunk, the food on the plates was not finished; and, as a crowning touch, there hung on the wall a first-class specimen of a Prussian Guardsman's helmet.

"They seem to have left in a hurry," remarked Tremayne, after a long inspection. "And that looks to me quite a pleasing specimen of helmet."

"Which, for God's sake, don't touch!"

The sudden voice from behind made him swing round, and there, framed in the doorway, stood the Sapper officer. Tremayne's hand dropped to his side, and he looked at the engineer stupidly.

"What on earth do you mean, old boy?" he said at length. "It's a damned nice helmet."

"Quite too nice to have been left here, however hurried the departure," rejoined the other. "Of course I may be wrong, but you know what happened yesterday."

"Good Lord! Do you mean that this house may be mined, too?" cried the adjutant.

But the Sapper took no notice. Standing on a chair, with his cheek pressed against the wall, he was peering behind the helmet. It was hanging by the strap on a big nail, so that the bottom of the helmet was against the wall, and the top swung out about an inch from the head of the nail. For a few seconds he examined it, and then he smiled gently.

"From a professional and from an artistic point of view, I congratulate the bird who did this. By Jove, Peter, my boy, the South Devons very nearly lost their adjutant and their billeting officer this morning."

"What do you mean, Sapper?" The adjutant was smoking a little faster than usual.

"That that is about the best booby-trap I've heard of yet." The engineer produced a pair of wire-cutters from his pocket, and they watched him insert them carefully behind the helmet. There was a snip, and they saw him lift the helmet off gingerly. Then he got down off the chair, and laid it on the table. "Very neat – very neat, indeed!"

"What's neat?" snapped Tremayne. "You bally specialists are so confoundedly cold-blooded."

The Sapper grinned.

"You see that wire sticking out of the wall there below the nail? That's the wire I cut – you can see the base end of it here made fast to the helmet. Now that helmet was hung by its strap, and its top was away from the nail. Supposing you had lifted it off, Peter, from the floor, you would have caught hold of the lower part, and in doing so would have pulled it away from the wall. The helmet would have pivoted round the strap, and the top part would have gone nearer the wall – would have touched the nail, in fact. After that the subsequent proceedings would have interested you no more."

"You mean that the helmet touching the nail would have completed the circuit?"

"Precisely. And the quickest way at the present moment in which you could deprive His Majesty's Army of the services of three particularly brilliant officers would be to touch the nail with the end of the wire sticking out of the wall."

"Thank you; it's all very interesting." Tremayne's face was set and hard. "Why can't the damned swine fight like gentlemen?"

"For the very good reason that they don't know how a gentleman fights." The Sapper rose and stretched himself. "I will just remove a little more of that wire to make things safe, and then I shall have no objection to lunching with you."

"But you aren't going to leave the place full of explosive, are you?" The adjutant paused at the door in surprise.

"My minions shall deal with the matter this afternoon," answered the engineer. "Everything is quite safe," he continued, as they passed into the street. "There's no delay action about this like yesterday. It's just a booby-trap pure and simple."

"Which unpleasantly nearly caught the booby," remarked Tremayne quietly. "It's devilish lucky, old man, that you were going round when you were. Otherwise – "

But it was unnecessary to finish the alternative.

Despite all assurances on the part of the engineer officer, the headquarters of the South Devons declined, as one man, to move their residence.

"It may," remarked the CO, "be all that you say and more, but I personally decline to chance it."

"Right-ho, sir!" laughed the Sapper. "The stuff is all removed, but if you don't like the idea – "

"I do not!" answered the Colonel firmly. "I am of a nervous disposition, and I grow more frightened daily. I refuse to place my valise in a munition works."

It was the following morning, and the two men were standing outside the door of the South Devons' mess.

"It's a dirty method of fighting," went on the CO after a moment. "Poor old Grayson" – he mentioned the late Colonel of the Loamshires – "and Finlayson, and all these others. And yesterday, but for the grace of God, and you being there, Tremayne and Hugh – " He stopped, and stared thoughtfully down the road. "Hallo, some prisoners! And an officer, too. Wonder what he is?"

"I think he's an engineer," answered the Sapper, inspecting his uniform. "Let's ask him."

Six shambling Huns, with a morose and scowling officer at their head, came to a halt in front of the Colonel, and the escort, a young and grinning Tommy, saluted.

"Told to bring this little bunch 'ere, sir," he remarked. " 'E ain't 'arf a little pet, that there one in front."

"Told to bring them here?" said the Colonel. "But they ought to go on to Brigade or Division. There's no cage here."

The Tommy scratched his head and looked blank. "This is where they said, sir," he repeated. "I don't know my way, sir, neither, not no farther – "

"All right, lad. I'll take them over from you. Hand them over to the sergeant-major, and the adjutant will sign your receipt."

"Come on, yer little bundles of beauty!" The Tommy sloped arms, and the party was preparing to move off, when the officer stepped forward.

All the time the Colonel was speaking his eyes had been roving up and down the street of the village. Once, when he caught the Sapper looking at him fixedly, he had scowled furtively and immediately turned away. He was a man of striking appearance, tall and broad, with a long red scar running across his right cheek. He seemed to be trying to hide that scar by turning up the collar of his greatcoat and getting well inside it; but whenever he moved or turned his head the top of it showed above his uniform.

"I would request," he said in a harsh voice, "to be separated from the soldiers, and sent on at once."

"You will be sent on when I wish," answered the Colonel, "and when it is convenient for me to send an escort to take you. You are an engineer officer, are you not?"

"I am; and I desire – "

But he got no further with the statement of his wishes. In speaking, he had thrown back his head, so that the whole of the scar was visible, and immediately an excited clamouring broke out in the little crowd of villagers and children which had collected. A score of fingers were pointed accusingly at the mark on his face, and everybody talked at once.

"There seems to be some slight upheaval," remarked the Sapper, glancing first at the scowling officer and the six impassive soldiers behind him, and then at the gesticulating villagers. "I will elucidate."

It was not a rapid matter, that elucidation. The crowd were all very anxious to speak, and proceeded to do so at the tops of their voices and the same time. But at last one fact emerged from the general din – a fact which caused the elucidator to become extremely thoughtful.

"They say, sir," he said, turning to the Colonel, "that this officer lived in this village for nearly two months just before the Germans left. They recognise that scar."

"I don't quite see what the devil all the excitement is about, even if he did," answered the Colonel. "It merely seems a strange coincidence."

"Yes. But they say he lived in the house where the Loamshires were." The two men looked at one another, and a light dawned slowly in the Colonel's face.

"The deuce, he did! And the blighter is an engineer."

"As you say – the blighter is an engineer."

They had been speaking in an undertone, but now the Colonel turned to the German officer.

"They say that you were billeted in this village before you evacuated it."

"I was."

"They say, moreover, that you lived in the house up there, which you now see is a heap of bricks."

For one moment and one moment only there flashed across the German's face a look of triumph; then it resumed its look of morose sullenness.

"I was; I suppose it has since been hit by a shell."

The Colonel was about to speak again when the Sapper caught his arm.

"Send him away, sir!" he whispered. "Send him away, but keep him in the village for a bit. I've had a brainstorm."

For a moment the Colonel hesitated.

"Didn't you see that look on the swine's face," urged the Sapper, "when he saw what had happened. I know he's the man – I'm absolutely certain of it!"

"Still, what the devil can we do?" The Colonel was still in doubt. "Even if he is – "

The Sapper interrupted him.

"Of course we can do nothing, sir; of course not. But it would be nice to know for certain; very nice to know." He was looking straight at the Hun as he spoke, and he was thinking of the doctor of the Loamshires. The doctor had been a great pal of his.

"Take 'em away," said the Colonel to the escorting Tommy. "I'll make arrangements later."

The party moved down the street, and he turned to the Sapper.

"What's in your head, old boy? I'd like to string that swab to a lamp-post; but I'd like to do lots of things I can't!"

"My dear Colonel!" The other held up his hands in horror. "The idea of such a thing! He must be treated in every respect like the gallant, merry hero that he is. In – er – every respect. Good morning, sir. I'll come and look you up in about two hours."

To say that he winked would be libellous; his eyelid fluttered slightly, but it was entirely due to the wind. So what it was that day at luncheon which caused the Colonel when he had finished telling the incident to add a postscript about "Greek meeting Greek" is, I regret to state, beyond me.

The meal was hardly over when the sapper walked into the mess, to be pounced upon immediately by Peter Tremayne.

"What have you found out?" he cried. "Is that the swine who did it?"

"My dear Peter," returned the engineer, "you outrage my feelings. I have been engaged in a couple of hours of – er – quiet study. In my branch of the army, you know, continual work is – "

"Dry up, you damned fool." Tremayne's face was set. "I'm in no mood for fooling. Is that the man who murdered Jimmy?"

"That is what I propose to find out now. Not exactly ordeal by fire, you know; but a sort of reconstruction of the crime. It might be amusing, and it will clear the air and remove doubts."

The Sapper lit a cigarette. "I want you to interview the prisoner, Colonel, in that room in which the booby-trap was put."

The South Devons looked at him in silence.

"What's the game?" remarked the adjutant shortly.

"None. Why should there be?" He thoughtfully blew out a cloud of smoke. "I shall be there myself, and don't be surprised or – er – alarmed at anything you see me do."

"What do I say to him?" asked the Colonel.

"Oh, any old thing! Ask after Hindenburg's health, and put him at his ease. I want him to think that you are using the place as your mess. I shall come in after he is in the room, and it won't take ten minutes." The Sapper grinned at them gently. "Shall we process?"

They rose and trooped over to the house in which the Sapper had found Tremayne and the adjutant the preceding day, and sat down round the table. Orders had already been sent for the prisoner, and in silence they awaited his coming.

"I see you've put the helmet back in position," said Tremayne. "I hope to Heaven you've removed the juice!"

"What do you think, papa?" laughed the Sapper. "In the words of an enterprising weekly – watch that helmet!" He glanced through the window. "Here he comes. Watch him, too!"

Now there rests over the last phase of this episode of Divine retribution a certain haziness – almost, one might say, the fog of war. The Hun came into the room and, according to Tremayne, the click of his eyes as they fastened on the helmet might have been heard down the street. But let me quote that veracious raconteur, as we got it later in the oyster shop at Amiens:

"There we all were sitting round the table, pretending to toy with some remnants of bad sausage and a glass of flat beer, when in walks Master Hun with the escort behind. He looked round the room once or twice, and then he spotted the Guardsman's helmet hanging upon the wall, just as it had been the day before. He got that helmet transfixed with such a gaze that he didn't even hear the Colonel's first question, and you can bet your shirt we weren't missing that loving look of his. Seen it before? Of course he'd seen it before. Why, the swine had put it there; he was the swab who'd caused all the trouble. I knew it, so did everyone.

"The play sort of dragged a bit, owing to the Hun missing his cue twice in his conversation. He couldn't talk and think about that helmet at the same time, with the nice little packet of trouble which he thought was underneath the floor, and I was just on the point of butting in with a leading question or two, when in strolls the Sapper – just as if he'd never seen us before. The Hun looked at him quickly and he looked at the Hun – and somehow I don't think they liked one another very much. The doctor man in the Loamshires – Jerry Dermot – and the Sapper had been great pals." Tremayne thoughtfully skewered an oyster, and contemplated it.

"However," he continued, "we were most of us wise to his game by this time, and, 'pon my soul, he acted well. Someone ought to write a play round that situation as a plot."

"Someone has," pessimistically barked an intense officer opposite, "and it's been rejected by every manager in London."

Tremayne looked offended. "Damn it! you don't know what the situation is yet."

"The point is immaterial," boomed the intense one still more pessimistically. "I, personally, have written a play round every possible and impossible situation which can or cannot occur. They have all been rejected by every manager in London. Proceed."

"He passed the time of day with the Colonel, and hoped he wasn't interrupting anything official; he murmured inanities about our having a nice mess, and then – he saw the helmet. Now he was acting, and we were all acting, and it says something for our acting that the Hun never spotted us. There wasn't a man in that room who hadn't got one eye at least on that dirty Boche."

Tremayne finished his Chablis savagely.

"The Colonel asked him a question, and he didn't answer. He'd got his eyes set on the Sapper, and he couldn't move 'em, and we watched him sweat. The sapper strolled up to that helmet, and he examined it from all angles.

"'That's a damned good helmet,' he remarked casually, 'damned good. Prussian Guard, isn't it?' He put up his hand towards it, and there was a noise like a stillborn explosion from the Hun. The Sapper swung round and looked at him. 'By Jove!' he cried. 'What's the matter? You look quite faint.' Then we all looked at him openly, and the sweat was pouring off that man's face in two streams.

"'I am all right,' he said thickly; 'but I would not – I would not –' The words sort of died away in his throat, and he choked a bit."

"The scene undoubtedly has its dramatic possibilities," murmured the intense officer. "It is, I believe, an established fact that the fear of death is worse than death itself, though how the deuce anybody knows..." He relapsed into silence.

"We didn't rush matters," continued Tremayne. "The Sapper came away from that helmet, and the sweat ceased coming away from the Hun. Then he returned again, and so did the sweat. He put up his hand and he fingered that helmet, and he talked casually while he did so. I was sorry for him really, because he missed the Hun's face. And then, at last, he started to take it down, and as he did so, with one ghastly shout of 'Don't touch!' the Hun leaped for his arm and caught it. It was really very fine: a pretty sight... Madame – *encore des huîtres, s'il vous plait.*" Tremayne looked round the circle of faces and his eyes were gleaming... "The Sapper, an infuriated figure of outraged dignity: the Hun shaking like a bally jelly and still holding his arm.

"'What the devil do you mean?' roared the Sapper. 'Let go my arm at once, damn you!'

"The Hun mouthed and sweated, and we waited.

"'Let me get it down for you,' he got out at last. 'If you could lend me a pair of wire-cutters.' He paused, and didn't seem to like meeting anyone's eye.

"'May I ask,' said the Sapper, in a voice you could keep the fish on all the summer, 'why you require wire-cutters to take down a helmet hanging on the wall?'

"'The helmet is secured to the wall by a wire,' stuttered the Hun. 'You will have to cut it, and I thought you might damage it.'

"'You know this room, then – and this helmet?' The Colonel chipped into the conversation, and you know what his orderly-room voice can be like.

"'Yes,' answered the German. 'When I was here before, I used this room.'

"'Indeed!' remarked the Colonel. 'Well, since the officer wishes to take down the helmet for us, I see no reason against it.'

"In perfect silence the Sapper produced some wire-cutters, and handed them to the Boche, who clambered on to a chair and flattened his cheek against the wall exactly as the Sapper had done the day before. And then that worthy winked at us – just once.

"'It will help you if I pull the bottom out a bit,' he said quietly, and we saw him do so. I put it that way because the Hun did not. That helmet only had to move an inch, but during the time it took to do it the Hun moved about ten yards. Head first he dived into the corner – straight off his chair as if it was into water. Only, as it wasn't water but a good stone floor, he ceased to take any active interest in the proceedings for the next ten minutes."

Tremayne lit a cigarette.

"When he came to again the helmet was lying on the floor beside him, and the wall was blank except for the nail, as it had been the whole time. He opened his eyes and peered round, and from that moment no one of us spoke a word. He saw the helmet

– he looked at the wall; then he looked at us, and – understood. For a while he didn't understand – he thought something had gone wrong with the works; but then suddenly he did. One could tell the moment when it came to him, the certainty that we had known all along; the realisation that we had watched him sweat with terror over his own dud booby-trap, and finally stun himself in the agony of his fear."

"Did he say anything?" asked a cavalry man sitting opposite.

"Not a word. No more did we. We just watched him in silence, and after a bit he got up and tried to pull himself together. Then he went, with the escort behind him, and that was the end of it."

Peter Tremayne got up and started to put on his British warm. I remember he paused at the door for a moment before going out.

"I once saw a man accused of cheating at cards before a lot of people – and the accusation was true. He was a decent fellow, but he was short of cash – and I have never forgotten the look in his eyes. He blew his brains out that night. I once saw a fellow at school – a great hulking blighter – who was caught stealing money red-handed. He came up before us prefects, and I have not forgotten the look in *his* eyes, either. And if you combine 'em, and multiply 'em by ten, and then do it all over again, you may have a dim idea of the look in that German's eyes just before he passed out of the picture. So long, boys; hope I've not bored you."

CHAPTER 15

The passing of the seasick cow

"Good evening, Jonah! And how is life, old top?" The man I was dining with greeted an officer passing our table with a cheery smile. "Come and tear a cutlet with us."

The other paused and regarded the speaker coldly. "James," he remarked, "you forget yourself. I can endure your face in the club at Poperinghe, I can even dally awhile with you in the boot shop at Bethune; but to dine with you in London and listen to your port-laden views of life is a thing which I will not do. My time is too short, James, to waste on such as you."

"He has affected that style of conversation," remarked James sadly, to no one in particular, "ever since he came under the influence of love. Is she here tonight, Jonah, this unfortunate girl of whom you so often babble when you are in your cups?"

"For what other reason would I have put on my new thirty-shilling suiting? Of course she's here, old boy; look – there she is coming down the steps. Some girl, Jimmy – what?"

He moved away to meet her, and with a nod and a grin to us came back past our table on the way to his own. As he said, she was "some" girl, and our eyes followed them both as they threaded their way through the diners.

"Who's your pal, James?" I asked him, when the girl had disappeared round the corner. "His views on the suitable companionship at face-feeding times commend themselves to me at first sight."

He ignored the implication, and concentrated on the tournedos for a while. Then suddenly he leaned back in his chair, stuffed his hands in his pockets, and contemplated me benignly.

"Peter," he remarked, "you are a lucky man. I am going to tell you a story."

"Great Scott!" I exclaimed; "not that long one about the girl and the lodging-house? You told me that last time I saw you, and got it wrong."

"What a mind you have, Peter; what a mind. No, I am not going to tell you the story of the girl and the lodging-house, brilliantly witty though it is. I am going to tell you a story – a true story – about a Tank."

"Human or otherwise," I remarked pessimistically.

James looked at me in pained surprise. "I am sorry to disappoint you: but – otherwise. Waiter – another bottle of champagne; the gentleman's thoughts have liquefied as usual."

He thoughtfully drained his own glass and lit a cigarette. "I have no objection to your eating while I smoke," he remarked kindly; "and a cigarette enables me to collect my thoughts and present to you my story in that well-known style on which my fame as a raconteur is largely based."

"Well, just write down the point before you forget it, or – "

"Once upon a time, Peter," he commenced, in a withering tone, "the Belgians made Ypres, and the Lord made the country around it. By Jove! there's little Kitty Drayton. I must go and speak to her afterwards."

"Yes, I'd tell her of your monumental discovery if I were you. Your reputation as a conversationalist will be made for life."

After a depressing interlude, during which he failed signally to catch the lady's eye, he again turned his attention to me.

"At a later period the Hun intervened. I believe you saw much of his earlier endeavours, Peter, around that delectable spot?"

"I did; moreover, I have since revisited the haunts of my youth. I don't mind telling you, James, that I had a devilish near squeak – "

"And if I'm not too bored I might possibly listen – later, but not now; at present, it's my story, and it's very rude to interrupt. You may say yes or no, Peter, if your feelings overcome you; otherwise, kindly restrain yourself."

He once again endeavoured to catch the wandering optic of fair Kate, with the same result as before; a bad starter at any time is James, but he frequently finishes well.

"The story which I am going to tell you concerns Wipers, in that it took place there or thereabouts. North-east of it, round about that cheerful little inland health resort, St Julian. A nasty spot, Peter, a nasty spot."

"Personally, I confined myself principally to Hooge," I murmured. "But I accept your words without prejudice."

"So much for the locality. The conditions need not detain us. Just one enormous morass of filth and mud and water and shell-hole; just the ordinary sort of country only a bit worse, and everything as damnable as it could be. Ugh, horrible! Let us come to pleasant subjects – to wit, the Seasick Cow – the principal actor in the drama.

"The Seasick Cow," he silenced my frivolous interruption with a glance, "was, and for all I know is at the present moment, a Tank. On the other hand, it may quite possibly be scrap-iron, as the position in which it was last seen goes into the air twice hourly. That, however, is immaterial; what I want to tell you about is her last voyage, which was by way of being a bit of an epic.

"I suppose you've heard of the new Hun pill-boxes. They are nasty contrivances made of reinforced concrete, and are dotted promiscuous-like all over the front. When hit by a shell the entire performance moves back a little farther, and the garrison, having sorted the sausage out of the mix-up, resume their interrupted breakfast two or three feet nearer Berlin. It was up against a little nest of these that the Powers that Be decided to do a bit of a strafe. They told off the Feet who were to be the proud and delighted performers and they gave 'em the Seasick Cow to help 'em. Then they gave them their blessing, and retired to await developments.

"Now the Cow was apparently *the* Tank of the Section. The whole crush are most inordinately proud of their machines, and spend hours in titivating up the interior; when I went inside the Cow once, her detachment had fairly spread themselves. The engine shone till you could see your face in it, and a Kirchner picture over the driver's head helped him to keep his eyes in the boat. Parts of her had been painted blue with a delicate motif of purple, and one only wanted a hat-rack and a bath in the corner to have the ideal weekend cottage."

"Your picture," I murmured, "is most explicit."

"All my pictures always are." James frowned absently at a passing waiter. "Have you ever been inside a Tank, Peter?"

"Once," I answered reminiscently, "after a heavy lunch. The Army Council stood outside and applauded, whilst I – "

"Army Council!" James interrupted me in his most withering tone. "Then it was in England you did the deed?"

"Where else," I returned, "would you expect to find the – ? But, hush! We are observed. Yes, it was in England – many moons ago, when I was on leave, that – "

"I am quite certain the story is immoral, so I won't trouble you any more. All I wanted to know before I really began was if you knew what the inside of a Tank was like. Apparently you do, so I will continue. A little '65 brandy, waiter, and a cigar."

James settled himself comfortably in his chair, and inspected his liqueur with the eye of a connoisseur. "One can't get it in France, you know, this stuff. I never can make out why not. However, Peter – having got past your digressions, let us proceed.

"The line, at the particular spot where this drama of the Seasick Cow was enacted, was in a state of flux. You know the sort of thing I mean: no man knows what his next-door neighbour doeth, but is merely the proud possessor of a shell-hole, water-logged, mark one. In the course of a previous operation we had captured the Green line, or the Blue line, or some bally line – I forget which: and our outposts had consolidated themselves – I don't think – in the unprepossessing piece of country in front. Which merely meant that A Company – much against its will – sat in slush and great peril one hundred and fifty yards nearer the Hun than anyone else. Now for the Hun.

"Away in front, three or four hundred yards on A Company's right, there rose a little mound, and beyond the mound, which was really the end of a sort of small spur, was a small valley. At the other side of the valley was another little hillock with the remnants of a farm on top... All right, Adolphus: my friend will pay for any damage I do to the tablecloth."

James shooed away a waiter, who was raising protesting hands to Heaven at the deep gouges in the cloth, by means of which my friend was endeavouring to show me the run of the ground.

"A valley crossing your front," I repeated, "screened from view by a small spur. And the principle of defensive war is the counter-attack."

"Clever boy!" James beamed upon me. "Why you aren't Commander-in-Chief has always been one of life's little mysteries as far as I am concerned. But there was something else, Peter: between the little spur and the hillock with the farm-house, and right at the very entrance to the valley, were a couple of pill-boxes. Do you take the situation?"

"With exactitude," I answered. "Process."

"This was the little bundle of fun which the Seasick Cow in company with the Feet were detailed to attack, hold, and consolidate."

"The answer," I remarked gently, "being a lemon. I always like to hear of these things after they've happened, and the band is playing, and the women are beautiful. If that wretched girl does happen to see you looking like that by any chance, and complains to the man with her, I will not be your second. My sympathies are all with her."

James came-to from his third frenzied endeavour on the unconscious Kitty and looked hurt.

"If there is one thing I loathe," he said coldly, "it's jealousy. However," he went on after a moment, "that was not all they were told to do. It was thought that fresh vistas would open before their delighted gaze, once they were the proud possessors of that valley, and further developments were left to the initiative of all concerned."

"Which makes it two lemons." I looked at James sternly. "Cut the tackle, my lad, and get to the 'osses. It's closing time here for all officers shortly, and we have foolishly forgotten to come in mufti. No chance of pretending we're on any important war-work."

"True, Peter; true. At times you're quite bright. I will get down to it. At 3.30 ak emma on a murky morning in August, *la belle vache* sogged wearily forward. She ploughed through shell-holes, and she squattered over mud, and generally behaved in the manner of all Tanks. She passed through A Company, and A Company waved her on her way rejoicing – they were not the party detailed to go with her; and in a few minutes she had disappeared from view in front. Once or twice her machine guns pattered out their joyful note, as they discovered a wily Boche lurking in a shell-hole; a bomb or two burst viciously in the dawn, but the old Cow sogged gently on. Then some Feet came through A Company – a party of the force detailed to act with the Tank, and from then on the usual confusion prevailed. Moreover, Peter, my story is now largely hearsay – though from much evidence, I can guarantee its truth. I think I will give it to you from the point of view of the crew of the Cow."

"Just on time, gentlemen. Any more liqueurs?" A solicitous waiter hovered around our table.

"Of course," I answered. "Make them double ones. Knowing this officer, I'm afraid it may be a long business. Now, James, as Tank Commander – carry on."

"The first thing the Cow encountered, bar a passing machine-gunner or two, whom they dispatched rapidly to a better, or, at any rate, less muddy world, was a pill-box. That was the one on the near side of the valley just beyond the first spur. Sport poor. The garrison ran like hell, and the light was too bad for good shooting. Only one man was caught for certain, and he slipped in endeavouring to negotiate a shell-hole. He slipped, as I said, and so did the Cow on top of him. A sticky end." James meditatively sipped his brandy: and we pondered.

"Then the Cow passed on. The arrangement was that she should make good the pill-boxes, and should then advance up the valley behind the infantry. But, unfortunately, mundane trifles intervened. Halfway between the two pill-boxes she stuck. In the vernacular she got bellied, and her infuriated crew realised that only extensive digging operations *from the outside* would save the situation. Which was annoying considering the fact that they were well within the German lines, and had so far sent only ten Huns to account for their nefarious past.

"However, there was nothing for it, and so the crew watched the Feet go past them, and they got out to investigate. And they were still investigating when a couple of hours later the infantry started to come back. Life, so the Tank Commander gathered, had not been all it might, two or three hundred yards farther on; more pill-boxes had appeared, with machine-guns placed in cunning nooks, and altogether the place was too hot for comfort. So, seeing that the operation was only a local one, the infantry officer in charge had decided quite rightly to withdraw, in order to save further useless loss of life.

"You get the picture, Peter!" James leaned forward with his eyes on me. "Trickling back slowly – the infantry; bellied and stuck – the Tank, a quarter of a mile in front of our own lines. Time – 6 a.m. on a summer's morning."

"Pleasant," I answered. "What was the Hun doing?"

"At the moment – not much. There was a lot of machine-gunfire in front, but practically no artillery. Then suddenly down came the barrage, and the Tank's crew hurriedly ceased their investigations and got inside. When they looked out again what was left of the infantry had disappeared."

"So," I said, "if I take the situation correctly, at the period we have got to at present, we have Tanks, one, disabled, with crew, a quarter of a mile odd in front of our outpost line, squatting at the point where a small hidden valley running across our front debouched into the open. Given in addition that the valley was obviously made for the massing of a counter-attack, and that one might reasonably be expected in the near future, we have all the setting for what our old pal Falstaff would have described as 'indeed a bloody business.' Don't interrupt me, James; I know it wasn't Falstaff, but he might just as easily have said it as anyone else. Question; What did A do – A being the Tank Commander?"

"When you've quite finished, I propose to tell you. And before I begin, what would you have done?"

"Hopped it like h – er – that is, I should immediately have beaten a strategic retreat, and reported to the man farthest in rear who would listen to me that I had, with deep regret, left the Seasick Cow bellied in the Hun lines, and please might I go on leave?"

"And no bad judge, either. But not so the Tank wallah, Peter, not so – but far otherwise. It may have seemed to you that up to date I have been speaking with undue flippancy; I'll cut it now, old man, for what I'm going to tell you is absolutely great. At 8 a.m. then, on a certain morning – the barrage being over – that Tank Commander found himself deserted. In front of him an occasional Hun dodged from shell-hole to shell-hole, but taking it all the way round there was peace. Behind him were his own people, but having bellied in a little fold in the ground, he was out of sight from them. And there was a counter-attack expected. So he called together his warriors and told them the situation; then they sat down and waited. He whose soul lay in the engines continued to polish them mechanically; the paint artist removed dirt from his handiwork and cursed fluently – while the remainder breakfasted on bully. Then they waited again.

"'If they start massing,' were the Tank Commander's orders, 'pop outside with the guns, get them into shell-holes, and let 'em have it. Then get back inside.'

"At midday the Hun put down a barrage on our own front line, and almost at once their infantry started massing in the valley. They came on in line of small columns, paying not the slightest attention to the Tank, which they thought was deserted. A beautiful target, Peter, one to dream about. From about a hundred yards did our cheery warriors open fire, and allowing for exaggeration, the bag was about two hundred. So that counter-attack did not materialise, and the crew had dinner.

"But now the whole aspect of affairs had changed, for the Huns knew that the Tank was very far from deserted. Given a good sniper, unlimited time, and ammunition, and a hole to shoot at, however small, sooner or later he will get it. It was about four o'clock that the monotonous ping-ping of bullets on the Cow's hide changed to a whistling flop, and with a drunken gurgle the painter crashed down on to the floor, and lay there drumming with his heels. Ten minutes later he died, and the crew had tea.

"Thereafter there was silence. Occasionally one of the men sitting motionless at his gun got in a shot at a fleeting target; but gradually dusk came on, the half-light time when one fancies things, when the bushes move and the hummocks of mud crawl with men. Then came the night.

"At 9 p.m. the Tank Commander had decided to send an NCO back to our lines to inform them of the situation; and at 9 p.m. therefore, the door was carefully opened, and a sergeant descended into the darkness. The next instant there was a guttural curse and a snarling, worrying noise. He had fallen on top of a Hun, and had only just time to stick a bayonet through his throat and jump back into the Tank again, and batten down the door when the Boches were all over them. For six long weary hours did they clamber over that Tank, bursting bombs on the top, trying to fire through loop-holes, shouting to the crew to surrender. And the only answer they got was: 'For heaven's sake go away: we can't sleep.' One proud Berlin butcher planted a machine-gun a yard from the door, and fired at it point-blank for an hour. Result – *nil*; except that just as he was going away, being a-weary of his pastime, his head coincided with the muzzle of one of the bigger guns of the Seasick Cow. A nasty death – though quick. And the evening and the morning were the first day.

"Twenty-four hours, Peter, up to date – quite enough, one would think, for the ordinary man. But not so for that Tank Commander. When the first chinks of light came stealing in through the loopholes, he took stock of his surroundings. Men can't go on firing point-blank through a Tank for six odd hours without doing some damage; and though a cautious survey of the ground outside revealed a pretty bag of dead and dying Huns, a continuous groaning from the corner by the engine showed that there was trouble inside as well. The groaning came from the sergeant, who had got the splinter of a bomb in the stomach, and across his legs lay another of the crew stone dead, shot through the heart. The polisher of engines was morosely nursing a right hand which hung down limply and dripped, and yet another had taken a bullet through the shoulder.

"'Boys,' remarked the Tank Commander, 'things have looked better – sometimes. But – they may put up another counter-attack today. What say you? Shall we pad the hoof?'

"'An' let them ruddy perishers 'ave the Cow? Not on your life, sir, not on your life.' The engineer scowled horribly. 'Besides, the boys may come back soon.'

"' 'Ear, 'ear.' The sergeant's voice was very feeble. 'Stick it out, sir, for Gawd's sake.'

"'Right you are, boys. Them's my sentiments. Let's have breakfast.'

"The next day was hot for a change – sweltering hot, and by the time the Boches put in another counter-attack the sergeant was delirious. It was a much more cautious affair this time, for they mistrusted that squat, silent machine. All the morning snipers had potted at her from three sides without effect, only the monotonous thud of the bullets lulled the remnants of the crew to sleep. It just requires a little imagination, Peter, that's all, to get the inside of that Tank. Two dead, one delirious, two more wounded, and – well, we will not specify further details. And brooding over all, an oppressive, sweltering heat, through which the sergeant moaned continuously and begged for water, while the others slept fitfully as best they could.

"Then came the second counter-attack. Once again the barrage on our own front lines roused the crew and they stood to their guns: once again they saw those small columns of Huns coming on. As I said, it was a far more cautious affair this one, and targets were hard to pick up; but they did pick 'em up, and for the second time the counter-attack failed to materialise. The thing which did not fail to materialise was an odd shot through one of the loopholes which found that a man's eye is not bullet-proof. And that made three dead…

"At dusk they held another council of war, and the Tank Commander gave tongue. 'Go forth,' he said, 'even like the penguins from the Ark and tell unto the Feet behind us that we are sore pressed, but that our tails – in so far as they remain – are in a vertical position, above our heads. Also that we have slaughtered large quantities of Huns, and would have them join us in this most exhilarating sport.'

"'Even so, O King,' spake out he of the wounded flipper, 'but who is to go? For upon casting my eye round the court circle, beside yourself there is but one unwounded man.'

"Forgive me thus bursting into language of rare beauty, but I'm afraid it's the brandy." James thoughtfully lit a cigarette. "I gather that words ran high in the Seasick Cow when the Commander insisted on the one unwounded man, accompanied by him of the damaged lunch-hooks, going back and leaving him. For a while they flatly refused to go, and it was not until he had sentenced them both to penal servitude for life that they reluctantly agreed to obey orders. And so at 8 pip emma on the second day they shook one another by the hand, grunted as is the manner of our race, and cautiously dropped out of the entrance and this story."

"Which up to date is not bad for you, James," I reassured him kindly.

"At the beginning of the second night, then," he continued coldly, "we find our Tank Commander practically alone. Three of his crew were dead, the sergeant unconscious, and the rest in varying stages of delirious babblings. And though it is easy to talk of here, yet if you will picture your own wanderings in No Man's Land, with the flares shooting up, and the things that were which jibber at you, and having pictured that, imagine yourself inside a Tank, with occasional shafts of ghostly light flooding through loopholes and shining on the set dead faces of the crew, I think you will agree that there are better ways of spending the night. Not a soul to speak to coherently: only one man who thought he was in Smithfield Market selling meat and monotonously called the prices, and another who was apparently playing mental golf round Westward Ho! Then, as a finale, the sergeant who occasionally came to and moaned for water; but being hit in the stomach, Peter, he couldn't have any. Those three and the dead…

"At 10 pip emma came the Huns again. They swarmed all over the Tank for the second time, and dodging from loophole to loophole was the Tank Commander. Sometimes he blew a man's head off from point blank range, sometimes a bullet whizzed past his own and ricocheted round the inside of the Cow. About twelve the golfer was hit through the heart, and shortly afterwards the Smithfield gentleman went clean crazy. He alternately fired a Verey pistol and one of the guns into the crowd outside, and, finding this too slow, endeavoured to open the door and charge. Then somewhat mercifully he collapsed suddenly and lay on the floor and babbled.

"About four next morning the Huns went away again, and the Tank Commander had just enough strength left to stagger to the gun and draw a bead on a stoutish officer some fifty yards away, who seemed very annoyed about something – probably the fact that the Cow was still there. He pulled the trigger, and the shell apparently burst on the officer; which must have been still more annoying for the poor man. Then with a short sigh of utter weariness he collapsed and slept. And the evening and the morning were the second day…

"About three o'clock the next day we went forward, preceded by a creeping barrage. Funnily enough, I personally found the mechanic and the other warrior. They had encountered a Hun patrol, and things had evidently moved. They were all dead – four Huns, and the two Tankites. The mechanic had apparently used a spanner with effect: he still had it gripped tight in his right hand. Then we went on and saw the Tank for the first time, because, being fresh troops, we knew nothing about it. It was dead – lifeless: but not so dead or lifeless as the mass of Germans heaped around it. The barrage reached it, played on it, and passed on; we reached it, looked at it, and were about to pass on when suddenly the door opened and a haggard-looking, blood-stained wreck appeared in it.

"'What a shindy!' he remarked. 'It's woken me up.'

"Lord, how the men laughed. It takes a lot to make anyone laugh who is trying to walk over Flanders, but they howled – he looked so confoundedly peevish. Then a couple of them looked inside the Tank and ceased laughing to be sick.

"'Got two stretcher-bearers?' asked the apparition. 'My sergeant's been hit in the stomach for forty-eight hours.'

"We found him two, and the last I saw of him for a few days he was wandering back with his sergeant through the filth. Met him often since at Poperinghe in the club, and at Bethune... Night-night, Jonah. When are you going back?"

"In five days, old boy. It's a hard life, is not it?"

Jonah and his girl passed slowly up the steps, and I watched them as they went.

"Poperinghe? Bethune!" I murmured slowly. "Is he the cause, by any chance, of your interesting but somewhat irrelevant yarn?"

As I spoke the glitter and scent, the lights and the women, seemed blotted out by another picture: a grim picture with a Tank for setting, a squat motionless Tank dripping with blood, surrounded by death.

"Of course," answered James briefly. "Three days and three nights in the belly of the whale: three days and two nights in the belly of the Tank.

"But, by Jove! there's Kitty on the move. Goodbye, old man. You might pay."

SAPPER

The Black Gang

Although the First World War is over, it seems that the hostilities are not, and when Captain Hugh 'Bulldog' Drummond discovers that a stint of bribery and blackmail is undermining England's democratic tradition, he forms the Black Gang, bent on tracking down the perpetrators of such plots. They set a trap to lure the criminal mastermind behind these subversive attacks to England, and all is going to plan until Bulldog Drummond accepts an invitation to tea at the Ritz with a charming American clergyman and his dowdy daughter.

Bulldog Drummond

'Demobilised officer, finding peace incredibly tedious, would welcome diversion. Legitimate, if possible; but crime, if of a comparatively humorous description, no objection. Excitement essential… Reply at once Box X10.'

Hungry for adventure following the First World War, Captain Hugh 'Bulldog' Drummond begins a career as the invincible protectorate of his country. His first reply comes from a beautiful young woman, who sends him racing off to investigate what at first looks like blackmail but turns out to be far more complicated and dangerous. The rescue of a kidnapped millionaire, found with his thumbs horribly mangled, leads Drummond to the discovery of a political conspiracy of awesome scope and villainy, masterminded by the ruthless Carl Peterson.

SAPPER

BULLDOG DRUMMOND AT BAY

While Hugh 'Bulldog' Drummond is staying in an old cottage for a peaceful few days duck-shooting, he is disturbed one night by the sound of men shouting, followed by a large stone that comes crashing through the window. When he goes outside to investigate, he finds a patch of blood in the road, and is questioned by two men who tell him that they are chasing a lunatic who has escaped from the nearby asylum. Drummond plays dumb, but is determined to investigate in his inimitable style when he discovers a cryptic message.

THE FEMALE OF THE SPECIES

Bulldog Drummond has slain his arch-enemy, Carl Peterson, but Peterson's mistress lives on and is intent on revenge. Drummond's wife vanishes, followed by a series of vicious traps set by a malicious adversary, which lead to a hair-raising chase across England, to a sinister house and a fantastic torture chamber modelled on Stonehenge, with its legend of human sacrifice.

SAPPER

THE FINAL COUNT

When Robin Gaunt, inventor of a terrifyingly powerful weapon of chemical warfare, goes missing, the police suspect that he has 'sold out' to the other side. But Bulldog Drummond is convinced of his innocence, and can think of only one man brutal enough to use the weapon to hold the world to ransom. Drummond receives an invitation to a sumptuous dinner dance aboard an airship that is to mark the beginning of his final battle for triumph.

THE RETURN OF BULLDOG DRUMMOND

While staying as a guest at Merridale Hall, Captain Hugh 'Bulldog' Drummond's peaceful repose is disturbed by a frantic young man who comes dashing into the house, trembling and begging for help. When two warders arrive, asking for a man named Morris – a notorious murderer who has escaped from Dartmoor – Drummond assures them that they are chasing the wrong man. In which case, who on earth is this terrified youngster?

OTHER TITLES BY SAPPER AVAILABLE DIRECT
FROM HOUSE OF STRATUS

Quantity		£	$(US)	$(CAN)	€
☐	ASK FOR RONALD STANDISH	6.99	11.50	15.99	11.50
☐	THE BLACK GANG	6.99	11.50	15.99	11.50
☐	BULLDOG DRUMMOND	6.99	11.50	15.99	11.50
☐	BULLDOG DRUMMOND AT BAY	6.99	11.50	15.99	11.50
☐	CHALLENGE	6.99	11.50	15.99	11.50
☐	THE DINNER CLUB	6.99	11.50	15.99	11.50
☐	THE FEMALE OF THE SPECIES	6.99	11.50	15.99	11.50
☐	THE FINAL COUNT	6.99	11.50	15.99	11.50
☐	FINGER OF FATE	6.99	11.50	15.99	11.50
☐	THE ISLAND OF TERROR	6.99	11.50	15.99	11.50
☐	JIM BRENT	6.99	11.50	15.99	11.50
☐	JIM MAITLAND	6.99	11.50	15.99	11.50
☐	KNOCK-OUT	6.99	11.50	15.99	11.50
☐	MUFTI	6.99	11.50	15.99	11.50
☐	THE RETURN OF BULLDOG DRUMMOND	6.99	11.50	15.99	11.50
☐	SERGEANT MICHAEL CASSIDY RE	6.99	11.50	15.99	11.50
☐	TEMPLE TOWER	6.99	11.50	15.99	11.50
☐	THE THIRD ROUND	6.99	11.50	15.99	11.50

ALL HOUSE OF STRATUS BOOKS ARE AVAILABLE FROM GOOD BOOKSHOPS
OR DIRECT FROM THE PUBLISHER:

Internet: www.houseofstratus.com including author interviews, reviews, features.

Email: sales@houseofstratus.com please quote author, title and credit card details.

Hotline: UK ONLY: 0800 169 1780, please quote author, title and credit card details.
INTERNATIONAL: +44 (0) 20 7494 6400, please quote author, title and credit card details.

Send to: House of Stratus Sales Department
24c Old Burlington Street
London
W1X 1RL
UK

Please allow for postage costs charged per order plus an amount per book as set out in the tables below:

	£(Sterling)	$(US)	$(CAN)	€(Euros)
Cost per order				
UK	2.00	3.00	4.50	3.30
Europe	3.00	4.50	6.75	5.00
North America	3.00	4.50	6.75	5.00
Rest of World	3.00	4.50	6.75	5.00
Additional cost per book				
UK	0.50	0.75	1.15	0.85
Europe	1.00	1.50	2.30	1.70
North America	2.00	3.00	4.60	3.40
Rest of World	2.50	3.75	5.75	4.25

PLEASE SEND CHEQUE, POSTAL ORDER (STERLING ONLY), EUROCHEQUE, OR INTERNATIONAL MONEY ORDER (PLEASE CIRCLE METHOD OF PAYMENT YOU WISH TO USE)
MAKE PAYABLE TO: STRATUS HOLDINGS plc

Cost of book(s): —————— Example: 3 x books at £6.99 each: £20.97

Cost of order: —————— Example: £2.00 (Delivery to UK address)

Additional cost per book: ————— Example: 3 x £0.50: £1.50

Order total including postage: ———— Example: £24.47

Please tick currency you wish to use and add total amount of order:

☐ £ (Sterling)　　☐ $ (US)　　☐ $ (CAN)　　☐ € (EUROS)

VISA, MASTERCARD, SWITCH, AMEX, SOLO, JCB:

☐☐☐☐☐☐☐☐☐☐☐☐☐☐☐☐☐☐☐☐

Issue number (Switch only):

☐☐☐

Start Date:　　　　　　**Expiry Date:**

☐☐ / ☐☐　　　　　　☐☐ / ☐☐

Signature: ——————————

NAME: ————————————————————

ADDRESS: ——————————————————

——————————————————

POSTCODE: ——————

Please allow 28 days for delivery.

Prices subject to change without notice.
Please tick box if you do not wish to receive any additional information. ☐

House of Stratus publishes many other titles in this genre; please check our website (**www.houseofstratus.com**) for more details.